Daphne's Secret

I called after Daphne, "Are you mad at me?"

Daphne spun around. "You just didn't want them to see you with me, did you?" Her face was full of hurt and anger.

I shook my head, but I couldn't deny it. "You don't understand, Daphne."

"Oh yes, I do." She glared at me. "I hate that school and I hate all the kids who go there. I'm never going back, never!"

"But Daphne," I said, "it's against the law not to go to school."

Daphne sighed. "You don't understand, Jessica. It's not just Tony and Scott and Michelle and the other kids. It's more than that."

"What is it? What's wrong?"

"If I tell you what's really wrong, will you promise not to tell anybody? Not your mother, or Mr. O'Brien, or anyone?" Daphne looked at me solemnly.

I nodded. "You can trust me," I whispered.

Daphne's Book

MARY DOWNING HAHN

A BANTAM SKYLARK BOOK®
TORONTO · NEW YORK · LONDON · SYDNEY · AUCKLAND

*This low-priced Bantam Book
has been completely reset in a typeface
designed for easy reading, and was printed
from new plates. It contains the complete
text of the original hard-cover edition.*
NOT ONE WORD HAS BEEN OMITTED.

RL 5, 009–012

DAPHNE'S BOOK

*A Bantam Book / published by arrangement with
Clarion Books*

Bantam Skylark edition / December 1985

*Skylark Books is a registered trademark of Bantam Books, Inc.
Registered in U.S. Patent and Trademark Office and elsewhere.*

ISBN 0-553-15360-9

Published simultaneously in the United States and Canada

Bantam Books are published by Bantam Books, Inc. Its trademark, consisting of the words "Bantam Books" and the por-
trayal of a rooster, is Registered in U.S. Patent and Trademark
Office and in other countries. Marca Registrada. Bantam
Books, Inc., 666 Fifth Avenue, New York, New York 10103.

PRINTED IN THE UNITED STATES OF AMERICA

CW   0 9 8 7 6 5 4 3 2 1

To my mother,
ELISABETH SHERWOOD DOWNING,
with love and affection

One

IT WAS ONE of those dreary January days when nothing goes right. First of all, I overslept. Then I discovered that my brother Josh had used up all the hot water taking his shower. And then, as a final blow, I saw Josh grab the last doughnut as he ran out the door.

By the time I was ready to leave for school, it was pouring rain. Anywhere else it would have been snow, but not here in Maryland. No, a blizzard was raging across New England, and I was sure that all the schools there were closed, but here I was, slogging down the footpath, my shoes soaked, my hair plastered to my forehead in wet strips. By the time I got to Oakcrest Middle School, I looked as if someone had dumped a bucket of water on me.

While I was trying to force my frozen fingers to open the lock on my locker, I dropped my lunch bag, and everything in it fell to the floor. Somebody stepped on my sandwich, and I never found my apple. I think Curtis Folwell probably ate it.

1

But all of these things were nothing compared to what happened in English. Mr. O'Brien, who used to be my favorite teacher, decided to ruin not only what was left of my day but my life as well. Not that I realized what he was up to at first. Oh no, I just sat there smiling innocently while he announced a new project for us.

"We have been invited to enter the seventh-grade Write-a-Book contest." Mr. O'Brien stroked his beard and smiled, inviting us to share his enthusiasm.

"We have to write a book?" Tony Cisco stared at Mr. O'Brien as if he had just announced that our class had been chosen to go on a forty-mile hike at the North Pole.

"A picture book, to be exact," Mr. O'Brien said.

As kids all over the room began protesting that they couldn't draw, hated drawing, didn't know how to write, etc., etc., etc., Mr. O'Brien somehow managed to regain control of the situation. "This is the way it works," he said. "You form teams. One writes the story, and the other illustrates it. Then you bind it like a real book. There's so much talent in this room that I know we can produce a winner."

"That's all there is to it?" Tony looked at Mr. O'Brien suspiciously.

"Well, it has to be between ten and twenty pages long, it has to be original, and spelling, punctuation, and neatness count." Mr. O'Brien smiled and shrugged. "It's going to be a great experience."

"Oh, man." Tony slumped in his seat, obviously depressed at the thought of punctuation and spelling. "Can't it just be pictures? No words, no sentences, no commas and periods and all that stuff?"

A little laugh rippled around the room, proving, as

2

usual, that the dumber you act, the funnier people think you are. But not people like Mr. O'Brien. He shook his head and frowned at Tony.

Gesturing for us to be quiet, Mr. O'Brien went on. "Since the books are team efforts, I've gone ahead and picked partners." As the class began to ripple again, Mr. O'Brien shushed us a little more forcefully. "One thing I want to make clear before I read the names. . . ." He paused dramatically and looked at us.

"There will be no changes. The partner I assign you is the partner you will keep. I've given the teams a lot of thought, and I will not make any changes. So don't come running up to me after class begging me to let you be someone else's partner. No matter what your reason is, I will not change my mind."

Everybody shifted around and murmured, but we got quiet as he started to read the list. I looked at Tracy Atkins and crossed my fingers, hoping he'd let us work together. We've been friends since kindergarten, but lately she's been spending more and more time with Michelle Swanson and Sherry Hartman. I was sure that if we worked on a book together, we'd soon be as close as we used to be.

I should have known that the Write-a-Book contest wasn't going to turn out any better than the rest of the day. First of all, Mr. O'Brien assigned Tracy and Michelle to work together. They both gave a little squeal and grinned at each other, as if they could hardly wait to start planning their book. Feeling very disappointed, I slid down in my seat and glared at Mr. O'Brien's feet, barely listening until I heard my name paired with Daphne Woodleigh. I sat up then and stared at him in

3

disbelief. He couldn't have put Daphne and me together! Tracy shot me a look of sympathy, but Michelle rolled her eyes and giggled.

While Mr. O'Brien continued to describe the contest, I stared at my desk, trying not to cry. How could Mr. O'Brien have done such a horrible thing to me? He must know how much everybody hated Daphne, he must have noticed how strange she was. Cautiously I looked across the room at her.

There she sat, her long black hair falling down her back, hiding her face like a dark curtain. As usual, she was wearing one of her bizarre outfits. Two or three layers of baggy sweaters and blouses, a calf-length tiered skirt, dark tights, thick leg warmers, and ballerina slippers. It was the sort of outfit a fashion model might wear, but in a roomful of girls wearing Shetland sweaters and blue jeans, Daphne's clothes looked terribly out of place.

Her wardrobe was only part of her problem. Daphne had appeared at Oakcrest in September, about a week after school started, but, as far as I knew, she had never said one word to anybody. Not even a teacher. When Mr. O'Brien called on her in class, she never knew the question, let alone the answer. She spent all her time either reading a library book or drawing elaborate doodles all over her notebook paper.

Even stranger was her attitude toward the kids in our class. The day she walked into English, she didn't seem to notice that everyone was staring at her. She just stood there in front of the room looking at the floor while Mr. O'Brien introduced her. Tony pretended to misunderstand her name.

4

"Did you say her name is Daffy?" he asked, glancing at Scott and Michelle to see if they were amused. They were, of course.

The name Daffy stuck, and to make it worse, Tony added "Duck" as an afterthought. For weeks, he led all the other kids in a chorus of quacks whenever Daphne appeared, but she ignored them. After a while, most of them got bored. What fun was it to tease someone if it didn't bother her? Tony, Scott, Michelle, and Sherry, though, never gave up. They still called her Daffy and quacked when she glided past them, her nose in a book.

As I sat there pondering my future as Daphne's partner, Kim Barnes handed me a tiny folded-up piece of paper. It was a note from Tracy. "What are you going to *do*?!!! You *can't* be Daffy's partner!!!" it said. I looked across the room at Tracy and shrugged my shoulders. What could I do? Mr. O'Brien had made it clear there would be no changes.

When the bell rang, I gathered up my things hastily, wanting to get away from Mr. O'Brien as quickly as possible. I wasn't fast enough, though. As I passed his desk, he reached out and took my arm. "Can I talk to you a minute, Jessica?"

Unhappily I nodded my head.

After everyone had run off to the cafeteria, he cleared his throat. "You didn't look very happy about the choice of partners for the Write-a-Book contest," he said.

Staring at the tan tiles on the floor, I shook my head. I was afraid to say anything because I knew I was about to cry. My lips were getting shaky and my chin was wobbling, and my eyes were brimming with tears.

"You know why I want you and Daphne to work together?" Mr. O'Brien asked softly.

I shook my head again.

"You're the best writer in the class, and she's the best artist. Together you should produce a wonderful book." He paused, probably expecting me to say something. When I didn't, he added, "There was another reason, Jessica. I think you're a very sensitive person. I can't imagine your hurting someone or being unkind." He paused again, but I kept right on staring at the floor, at our shoes, his a pair of scuffed loafers, mine a still-damp pair of running shoes, both of them blurred by my tears.

"Daphne needs a friend, Jessica," he said, his hand on my shoulder. "Please give her a chance."

"I'll try," I whispered unhappily. Ever since the first day of English class, I'd liked Mr. O'Brien. Although I hadn't seen my real father for years, I often pretended that he was like Mr. O'Brien—handsome, patient, kind, and understanding. Now here was Mr. O'Brien telling me I was a sensitive person, the sort who could help a girl like Daphne. Even though I was sure I couldn't do a thing for her, I didn't want to let Mr. O'Brien down. If he thought I was sensitive, I would be sensitive.

"It's just that I wanted to be Tracy's partner. I thought we could make a good book together," I said, still hoping he might change his mind. Maybe he hadn't thought of Tracy and me as a team.

"I'm sure you and Tracy could do a good job, Jessica, but I think you and Daphne can create something really special. Okay?" He gave my shoulder a gentle little shake and smiled at me.

"Okay." I blinked hard, trying to rid my eyes of tears, and did my best to smile at him.

"Good girl. I knew I could count on you, Jessica." Releasing me, he smiled again. "Well, I didn't mean to take so much of your lunchtime. You better hurry on down to the cafeteria."

After I left Mr. O'Brien, I went to the girls' room instead of the cafeteria. Locking myself into a stall, I cried for several minutes. Then I sat there glumly reading the messages on the wall. "John and Susie 4-Ever!" "Michelle and Tony—TRUE LOVE!!!" And some other stuff about sex that I didn't understand and didn't want to understand.

Although I wasn't very hungry, I ate what was left of my sandwich, and then I waited for the bell to ring. I just wasn't up to sitting at a lunch table with Tracy, Michelle, and Sherry. I knew that all they'd talk about was Daphne, and I didn't feel like listening to it.

Two

By the time I got out of school, the rain had turned to a nasty, cold drizzle, and I plodded along the footpath, feeling as gloomy as the bare, dripping trees looked. Pausing on a bridge, I leaned over the rail and watched the creek go frothing and swirling over the rocks. Idly I dropped a twig in the water and saw it go dancing away on the current.

As I stood there shivering in the rain, I thought about what Mr. O'Brien had said. Did he think I was sensitive because I wore glasses and wrote the best compositions in class and always got A's on my tests? Or because I was shy and always hovering on the edge of things?

He probably realized that I wasn't what you would call a popular person. But I wasn't an outcast either. Kids like Michelle and Sherry tolerated me; they didn't hate me or make fun of me. They even let me sit at their lunch table.

But that was mainly because of Tracy. She was the

one who stood up for me. More than once she had defended me when Michelle or Tony took a pot shot at me for being so brainy or looking more like a nine-year-old than a twelve-year-old.

What would happen to me now that my name was linked to Daphne's? I shuddered, knowing I could never bear the sort of teasing she endured day after day. Daphne, strange as she was, was obviously a lot tougher than I was. The very thought of being laughed at made me tremble.

If I'd had more self-confidence, I probably wouldn't have worried about it. I would have told myself that it was just a school project with no bearing on my social life. But I had very little self-confidence, and I was sure that it wouldn't take much to turn people like Michelle and Sherry against me. I was afraid that by the time the Write-a-Book contest was over, I would be as friendless as Daphne.

Glumly I crossed the bridge and took a short cut through a field behind the townhouses. As I unlocked our front door, I heard Josh's stereo shaking the walls, filling the whole house with the sound of drums and electric guitars.

"Do you have to play that dumb music so loud?" I shouted.

"What?" Josh stuck his head out of the kitchen. He was stuffing a huge peanut butter and banana sandwich into his mouth and trying to talk around it.

"Turn your stereo down!"

"I will when I go upstairs. I have to hear it down here, don't I?" He poured himself a glass of milk and dumped half a can of chocolate syrup into it. "What's the matter, Jesso? You have a bad day at school or something?" He gave me a condescending smile and reached out to pat the top of my head.

Angrily I ducked away, scowling at him. Just because he's in the ninth grade, he thinks he can treat me like a little kid.

Taking a bite out of an apple, Josh looked down his long nose at me. "Just wait till you get to high school, kid. You'll appreciate Oakcrest then." Shaking his head, he wandered upstairs. His door thunked shut and the stereo dropped to a bearable thrum of drums and snarling singers.

I went into the living room, picked up Snuff, our cat, and collapsed on the couch. From where I lay, I could see the gray sky, the bare trees, and the upper stories of the row of townhouses behind ours. They were tan stucco, and the rain had covered them with streaks, making them look drearier than usual. Shutting my eyes, I decided that Adelphia was a boring and depressing place to live, full of boring and depressing people.

"You know what?" I said to Snuff, who was crouched miserably on my stomach, waiting for an opportunity to escape. "When I'm sixteen I'm going to quit school and hitchhike around the world. I'm going to places like Tibet and New Zealand and Laos and Thailand, and I'm going to write about them and take all kinds of pictures. My articles will be in the *National Geographic*, Snuff. I'll win a Pulitzer Prize, and Mr. O'Brien will be so proud of me."

As Snuff wiggled frantically, trying to get away from me, I imagined myself squatting in a rubble-strewn street somewhere in the Near East, photographing an approaching tank or saving a dying child.

Unimpressed by my future, Snuff flattened her ears and hissed. Then, digging her claws into my sweater, she made a supreme effort and leaped from my arms.

"Just wait till I'm famous, you stupid cat! You'll be sorry then." Angrily I tossed a pillow at her, but she dodged it effortlessly and ran into the kitchen. I could hear her crunching away at her cat food, making herself fatter and fatter.

Around six o'clock, I heard the front door open. "Hi, I'm home," Mom shouted from the hallway. "Is anybody here?"

"I'm in the living room," I called, "And Josh is upstairs doing permanent and irreversible damage to his ears."

Mom came in and sat down on the end of the couch. "How was school today, Jess?"

I sat up and threw my arms around her. "It was awful, just awful!" Before she had a chance to say anything, I told her what Mr. O'Brien had done to me. "Everybody hates Daphne. They call her Daffy Duck and they quack whenever they see her. I don't want to be her partner, Mom!" Giving her another hug, I looked pleadingly at her. "Could you call up Mr. O'Brien and tell him how upset I am and ask him if he could please let me work with someone else? Please, Mom, please, could you?"

Mom looked at me, her face puzzled but not as sympathetic as I had hoped it would be. "Jessica, I'm sorry you're so unhappy about this, but I'm sure working with Daphne won't be as bad as you think it will."

11

She hugged me and gave me a kiss; her cheeks were still cold from being outside, but her arms made me feel warm and protected. "Did you put the casserole in the oven when you came home from school?"

"Oh no, I forgot all about it, Mom!" Stricken with guilt, I watched her take the Pyrex dish out of the refrigerator and stick it in the oven. "I'm sorry, Mom, I really am, but I was so upset about school, I just didn't think about it."

Slamming the oven door shut, Mom frowned at me. "I'm sorry, too, Jessica. I was expecting dinner to be almost ready when I got home."

I followed Mom out to the kitchen so I could continue our conversation about Mr. O'Brien and Daphne. As I watched her cleaning up the mess that Josh had left on the counter, though, I changed my mind. Without waiting to be asked, I got out the silverware and started setting the table. I had a feeling she might be in a better mood after dinner.

Later that night, I sat down on the couch next to Mom. She looked up from the book she was reading. "Did you finish your homework?" she asked.

I nodded. "I did all my math and I wrote my book report." Clearing my throat, I smiled at her. "You know the Write-a-Book contest I was telling you about?"

"It sounds like something you'd really enjoy doing. Do you have an idea for your story yet?"

"No, but I'll think of something. It's not due till February twentieth, so I have a whole month." I paused and started fiddling with the fringe on one of the throw pillows. "The thing is, I want to do it with Tracy. Not Daphne."

Mom stared at me. "What's so awful about Daphne?"

I screwed up my face, trying to figure out a way to explain someone like Daphne to my mother. "Well, she's really weird. She never does anything in school, and I know she won't do her share of the book." I paused. "Couldn't you ask Mr. O'Brien to let me be partners with Tracy?"

"Have you talked to him?"

I nodded. "But he won't let me change."

"I'm sure that Mr. O'Brien has a good reason for pairing you with Daphne. What did he say when you talked to him?"

I looked down at the pillow again. "He said I was the best writer and Daphne was the best artist, and he said I was a sensitive person and I should try to be Daphne's friend."

I sighed and leaned against Mom's side, letting her encircle me with her arm. "I don't want to hurt Daphne, Mom. I've never teased her or laughed at all the dumb jokes Tony and Michelle and Sherry make. I'm just scared that they'll tease me. I don't want Tracy to stop liking me. I don't want to be like Daphne."

"Oh, Jessica, nobody will hate you if you work with Daphne on a project." Mom hugged me. "Mr. O'Brien must think a lot of you, honey. Do as he says. Try to be friendly to Daphne. Put yourself in her place—imagine how lonely and unhappy she must be."

I looked at Mom sadly. "You just don't understand," I said. "You don't know how kids at Oakcrest are." Sighing deeply, I got up from the couch. "I think I'm going to go to bed, Mom."

She pulled me close and gave me a kiss. "Good night, Jess." Then she smiled. "Give her a chance, sweetie. Don't let Mr. O'Brien down."

Slowly I climbed the steps. Of course I didn't want to let Mr. O'Brien down. I couldn't help feeling pleased that he thought I was a nice person, and despite all the bad thoughts I was having about Daphne, I did wish I could help her. But at the same time, I knew I couldn't. Not if I wanted to keep Tracy as a friend. Not if I wanted to stay on Michelle's good side.

Three

THE NEXT MORNING it was still raining. Lying in bed, looking at the gloomy sky and bare branches outside my window, I wished I could stay home. I didn't want to go to school, I didn't want to see Michelle and Sherry, I didn't want to be Daphne's partner.

But as usual, Josh started banging on my door. "Rise and shine, Jess-o!" he croaked in his horrible half-changed voice. "It's another beautiful day."

"Shut up," I moaned. "Go away and leave me alone."I pulled the covers over my head, but nothing could muffle the sound of that voice.

"Doodle-dee-doot-de-do!" He trumpeted, his voice cracking and going up three octaves.

"Josh, stop that racket!" Mom yelled from downstairs. "And Jessica, you get up this minute!" she added, just to prove she didn't have any favorites.

"Okay, okay," I mumbled. Unlike Josh and Mom, I don't have the strength to yell first thing in the morning, not before breakfast anyway.

15

"And don't spend an hour in the bathroom," Josh said as I stumbled past him. "I haven't brushed my teeth yet."

Ignoring him, I slammed the bathroom door and turned on the shower, praying he'd left enough hot water for me this morning. By the time I finished blow-drying my hair, Josh was pounding on the door and shouting at me to hurry up.

Mom was finishing her coffee when I came downstairs. "What a horrible gray morning." She frowned at the rain falling endlessly from the cloudy sky.

"Just think, if it were snowing instead of raining, they'd close the schools," I said.

"But they wouldn't close the library," Mom said glumly. "Mr. Shepperd would expect me to be there even if we had ten-foot-high drifts blocking the roads." She sighed and got up to rinse her cup.

"Has anybody seen my English homework?" Josh ran into the kitchen, his red hair standing out in a halo of frizzy curls around his thin face. "I left it right there!" He pointed at an empty space on the kitchen counter. "Who moved it?"

"What's that?" I pointed at a messy pile of notebook paper heaped on the buffet.

"Well, *I* didn't leave it there." Josh scooped up the papers and stuffed them into a textbook already oozing sheaves of ragged assignments. "'Bye, Mom, 'Bye, Jess-o." He opened the door and let in a blast of icy air before slamming it behind him. As he passed the dining room window, hunched like a scarecrow in his dirty blue parka, he waved once more.

"Well, it's almost time for me to leave." Mom put her cup in the dishwasher. "Be sure and turn this on before you leave, Jessica. I don't think we have a single clean glass."

I watched her button her coat and put on her hat. "Have a nice day, Mom," I said.

"You too, honey." She gave me a quick kiss. "And try not to be so unhappy about the Write-a-Book thing."

I nodded. The door shut behind her and the house got very quiet. No radio or stereo blasting my ears, no Josh pounding up and down the stairs, no Mom bustling around. Just the refrigerator starting up and Snuff crunching her cat food.

I finished eating my cereal, rinsed my dishes, and put them in the dishwasher. Feeling responsible, I turned it on, glad that I'd remembered.

As I gathered up my books, Snuff stalked past me, jumped up on the couch, and curled herself into a contented little ball.

"You lucky cat." I bent over and scratched her behind the ears. She opened one eye and stared at me suspiciously, but she didn't leap up and run away.

"You can stay here all day, nice and dry and warm," I said enviously. "You have the whole house to yourself, and you can eat and sleep whenever you feel like it. You don't have to go out in the cold rain, you don't have to be Daphne's partner, you don't have to worry about people liking you. You really have a great life, you big fat furry monster you."

Snuff stretched and purred. She looked very smug, as if she understood every word I said.

17

Grabbing my parka, I opened the door. Ugh. It was even worse than yesterday. "Why can't you be snow?" I snarled at the raindrops.

In English, Mr. O'Brien started class by telling us he'd changed our seats so we could all sit next to our partners. Unhappily I picked up my books and moved to the desk beside Daphne, dropping everything with a thud so loud that Mr. O'Brien frowned at me. Daphne, of course, didn't even look up. She just sat there doodling on a piece of notebook paper, her long hair tumbling down and hiding her face.

"Let's get quiet now." Mr. O'Brien looked around the room. "I want to explain this assignment."

Passing out a dittoed bibliography, he told us that he was going to take us to the public library to look at picture books. "You should see some good examples before you start working on your own books."

Tony leaned back in his seat indignantly. "These are baby books. Why do we have to waste our time reading kid stuff?"

Everybody laughed, and a lot of kids started agreeing with Tony. Mr. O'Brien sighed and smoothed his beard. "I knew somebody was going to say that," he said. "In my opinion, most of these books are too good to limit them to little children. I think most of you will really enjoy looking at them." He paused and smiled at Tony. "But if you don't buy that, Tony, think of it this way. Each one is only about thirty-two pages long."

"That's probably more than Tony can handle," Mike DeSales said. "The longest book he ever read was the special anniversary Spiderman comic book. It couldn't have been more than twenty-four pages long."

"Yeah," Scott Turner added, "and it was mostly pictures. Except for the POW's and ZAPP's and OOOH's."

By now everybody was laughing, even Mr. O'Brien, and Tony was muttering, "Okay, okay. Big deal, man, big deal."

Curiously I shot a quick, sidewise look at Daphne, but she was still bent over her drawing as if she were on another planet. Her bibliography lay untouched on her desk, and she seemed completely indifferent to the laughter rippling around her.

"Well, enough for now about our books," Mr. O'Brien said. "Let's get back to the unit on paragraphing."

As Mr. O'Brien did his best to make his subject interesting, I slumped in my desk, staring at my textbook. I was too depressed to find the topic sentence in a boring paragraph about wheat production in Kansas. To tell the truth, I didn't care whether the paragraph had a topic sentence or not.

Although I tried not to think about Daphne, I was uncomfortably aware of her every time she shifted her position, coughed, sniffed, or sighed. The sound of her pencil scratching across her paper irritated me, and so did the sight of her foot, clad in black tights and a red Scholl sandal, swinging back and forth, catching my eye as it moved. When the bell rang, I jumped out of my desk, eager to get away from her.

"Don't forget, we go to the library tomorrow. Be sure to bring in your signed permission slip," Mr. O'Brien said as we all started for the door like a herd of cattle heading for the feeding trough.

Going down the hall to the cafeteria, I caught up

with Tracy. I managed to stick with her through the line and eased in beside her at the lunch table.

"Do you have an idea for your story yet?" Tracy asked me.

I shook my head. "I haven't really thought about it."

"Maybe you should find out what Daphne draws best and write about that," Tracy said.

"Ducks, Daffy draws ducks best!" Michelle almost choked on her milk, laughing and quacking at the same time.

"Did Tracy tell you what her and me are doing?" Michelle asked after she'd calmed down. "We're writing this story called 'The Nightmare Slumber Party.' It's about these girls who get killed one by one at this slumber party. It's really scary because they keep hearing these weird sounds and all these horrible things happen." Michelle paused and took a bite of her tuna fish sandwich.

"Like they step on this squishy thing, you know," she continued, "and they think it's a grape, but it's really an eyeball, and this girl gets her head cut off, and they find it hanging by its hair from the chandelier. All kinds of stuff like that happens, but in the end, just as the girl who's giving the party is about to be killed by this crazy man who escaped from the insane asylum, she wakes up and finds it was just a bad dream. It's a kind of surprise ending, you know?"

I glanced at Tracy, but she wasn't laughing and she didn't look embarrassed. "I've already started drawing some of the pictures," she said. She opened her notebook and pulled out a piece of paper. "This is going to be the cover."

She'd drawn five girls with huge chests and tiny waists like Barbie dolls. They were wearing tight jeans, high heels, lots of makeup, and perfect, flipped-back hair like Michelle's.

"But I thought it was supposed to be a picture book," I said.

"It's going to have plenty of pictures," Tracy said.

"And it's a lot more interesting than some dumb Jack-and-Jill story," Michelle said. "One of the girls is going to have a boyfriend who sings in a rock band and drives a red Camaro." She looked at me and shook her head. I knew Michelle was thinking I was incredibly naive.

"Only I can't draw cars," Tracy said.

"So Tony's going to draw the Camaro if Tracy draws the soldiers for his story," Michelle added. "Tony can draw jeeps and tanks and planes, but he can't draw people."

"Only I can't draw men very well," Tracy said. "They always look like girls with mustaches. I draw girls, flowers, and horses best."

"I don't think Tony's story is going to have any of those things in it." Michelle looked doubtful.

Before I could ask any more questions, the bell rang and we hurried off to biology to learn about the fascinating life cycle of the amoeba.

While Mrs. Kaufmann described the amoeba's style of reproduction (which Tony found hilarious), I doodled little geometric designs in the margin of my notebook

21

paper. Looking across the room, I noticed Daphne sitting a couple of rows away. Her head was turned toward the windows, and I wondered what she was thinking about.

It occurred to me that she probably wasn't any happier than I was at the prospect of our being partners. No doubt she thought I was just like all the other kids at Oakcrest. I tried to picture myself as she saw me. Just another girl in a Shetland sweater and blue jeans, following Tracy everywhere, too stuck up to speak to a person like Daphne. She'd probably never noticed I didn't quack or laugh at her.

Sighing, I stared at the picture of the amoeba in my textbook. Its life was certainly boring, virtually pointless, but at least it didn't have anything to worry about. No complex social problems beset the amoeba.

As Mrs. Kaufmann passed out dittoed sheets of questions about one-celled creatures, I glanced at Daphne again. Why did she look so sad? For a second, I found myself wishing I could see her smile at least once.

Four

THAT NIGHT I lay in bed worrying about the Write-a-Book contest. No matter how much I thought about it, I couldn't come up with a good idea.

What was the matter with me? I'd always thought of myself as a writer. In my closet were boxes full of stories I'd written, some of them dating back to the second grade, but none of them seemed good enough to haul out and rewrite.

Turning onto my back, I stared at the moon outside my window. The size of a quarter, its full face seemed to return my stare. "It must be Daphne's fault," I said to the moon. "If I had a different partner, I'd have my story all written by now. I know I would. And it would be good too. A lot better than 'The Nightmare Slumber Party.'"

I grimaced, thinking of Michelle sitting there at the lunch table, her mouth full of tuna fish, talking about her dumb story. She was such an idiot. How could Tracy stand her?

With a little thump, Snuff jumped up on my bed and walked up my legs. Stopping on my stomach, she stood there staring at me, kneading my blankets with her hard little paws. Stroking her, I coaxed a resistant purr out of her.

Just as I was starting to relax, Snuff hopped off my bed and stalked over to the closed door. She scratched at it and meowed plaintively. Reluctantly, I left my nice warm bed and let her out.

As I turned to go back to bed, I glanced at my dollhouse. In the moonlight it looked almost magical. Its roof was touched with silver, and its two towers cast sharp shadows on my bedroom wall. Picking my way through the shoes, books, and clothes heaped here and there on the floor, I knelt in front of the dollhouse and groped in the dark for the switch that illuminated its interior.

As the tiny chandeliers lit up the rooms, I saw that Snuff had been sleeping in the dollhouse, wedging her fat, furry body in among the little tables and chairs, scattering them about and leaving cat hair on the carpets.

Although my room was cold, I resisted the urge to go back to bed, and set to work straightening up the dollhouse. As I rearranged the furniture, I remembered the day last summer when Michelle and Tracy had caught me playing with the inhabitants of the house, a family of small stuffed mice that I had bought one by one at a crafts shop in the mall.

I had tried to convince them that I was redecorating the house, not *playing* with it, but they had teased me for weeks about it. I had been so embarrassed that I hadn't touched the dollhouse since.

When all the furniture, except for a few pieces that Snuff had broken, were in place, I began putting the mice in their favorite rooms. First, Princess Heatherfern. She belonged in the best bedroom, the one with the canopy bed and the bureau with tiny drawers that opened and shut. I stood her near the window, where the moonlight would touch her white fur and make her satin cape gleam.

Cragstar the Wizard was next. Up to the tower he went to stand peering into the fireplace, thinking of grand schemes and magical feats.

Into the cozy nursery went Baby Mouse and faithful Nurse Marigold, and up into the attic went the wicked witch Malvolia, the sworn enemy of Cragstone. There in the shadows she plotted deeds of evil.

But where was Sir Benjamin, my favorite mouse? Dressed in a blue velvet cape, wearing a plumed hat, and carrying a shiny sword, he was the guardian of the dollhouse. Without him, who would protect them from Malvolia?

Crawling around the floor, I looked under my bed, poked about under my bureau, rummaged through dirty clothes, pawed through shoes and books, and even risked my life by searching my closet. Nowhere did I see Sir Benjamin.

Sadly I left Princess Heatherfern keeping a lonely vigil at her window and crawled into bed. Undoubtedly Snuff had mistaken Sir Benjamin for a real mouse and dragged him away to some secluded spot. There she had probably torn him to shreds, velvet cape, plumed hat, and all. Rolling over on my side, I fell asleep promising myself to look for him in the morning.

"What were you doing up so late last night?" Mom asked me at breakfast. "I heard you moving around in your room after I'd gone to bed. It must have been midnight."

"I couldn't sleep, so I straightened up my dollhouse. Snuff got in it somehow and messed it all up."

"Oh, Jessie, don't let that miserable beast wreck your dollhouse. Your grandfather spent a lot of time making it, and I want you to take care of it."

I nodded, feeling bad. Grandfather had died four years ago, not long after he'd finished the dollhouse, and Mom and I both missed him a lot.

"Keep your door closed when you're not home so Snuff can't get into your room," Mom added.

"I will." I swallowed some orange juice. "Have you seen Sir Benjamin?"

"Who?" Mom looked puzzled.

"One of my little mice. The one with the plumed hat and sword."

She shook her head. "Can't you find him?"

"I think Snuff ate him or something."

"I could say something about cleaning your room, but I'll do my best to keep my mouth shut." Mom got up and put on her coat. "Have a nice day, sweetie. I have to go." Giving me a kiss, she left for work.

I finished my breakfast and read the comics and my horoscope. As usual, it predicted a dull day: I should visit someone in a hospital, I should heed a colleague's advice and sell my shares in a company owned by a Pisces, and I should avoid taking any transatlantic flights for the next two weeks. Realizing I'd wasted five minutes pondering the meaning of three sentences, I grabbed my parka and ran outside.

The rain and gray skies had disappeared, blown away by the wind that almost knocked me down as I cut across the parking lot. To make it worse, the temperature must have dropped twenty degrees. By the time I got to school, I was afraid to open my mouth for fear my face would crack.

"What a terrible day to go to the library," Michelle was saying as we walked down the hall to English. "My hair is just going to be all over my head, you know? I hate it when the wind blows and it's cold. I wish my father would get transferred to Florida or something. I mean I just can't take this weather."

Although I didn't say it, I wished Michelle's father would get transferred, too. To Alaska, maybe, or the South Pole. Some place far away where the wind would mess up Michelle's hair every day. Some place where she would be miserable and I would never have to see her again.

"Maybe Mr. O'Brien will make us walk with our partners." Michelle shot me a sly little smile.

"Oh, poor Jess!" Tracy said. "I hope he doesn't do that."

Luckily for me, Mr. O'Brien didn't say a word about partners. After all, we weren't in elementary school. So I walked along with Tracy and Michelle and Sherry, but for all the attention they paid to me I might as well have been invisible.

Not too far ahead, I saw Daphne walking all by herself, her head down as if she were watching her shadow

27

or something. The wind lifted her black hair in plumes and swirled it about, then dropped it down in ripples across the back of her dirty red parka. No matter what people thought about her, she certainly had the most beautiful hair I'd ever seen.

When we got to the library, I looked around for Mom. She was sitting at the Information Desk in the Adult Reading Room talking to a nice-looking old man. When she saw me, she smiled and waved.

"Who's that?" Sherry asked.

"My mother. She's a librarian here," I said, hoping Mom wouldn't do anything to embarrass me. I knew I'd die a thousand deaths if she were to come over and give me a big hug or something.

"No wonder you read so much." Sherry turned to Michelle. "Can I borrow your comb when you're done?"

As Michelle handed Sherry her comb, Mr. O'Brien herded us into the Children's Room and gathered us together. "Please get a table with your partner," he said, just as I was sitting down next to Tracy. "It's important that you work on this as a team."

Tracy smiled sympathetically at me, but Michelle said, "You better find another table, Jess. I don't want Daffy sitting here." Although she was laughing when she said it, I knew she wasn't kidding.

Reluctantly I got up and looked around the room for Daphne. I finally spotted her sitting at a small table all by herself in a corner. As I sat down across from her, she moved her hand to cover the picture she was drawing in her notebook. She didn't look up or say a word to me. We sat there as mute as two statues, waiting for Mr. O'Brien to tell us what to do.

The children's librarian had filled two book carts with picture books. Holding a couple of them up for us to see, Mr. O'Brien told us to take a few from the carts and examine them.

"Try to figure out what makes them good. Is it the pictures or the words, or is it both?" He smiled encouragingly. "Get some ideas for your own books, but don't copy. Your book has to be completely original."

Leaving Daphne sitting at the table, hunched over her drawing, I walked to the cart, selected a couple of books, and sat back down. Tony followed me, carrying two books. Dumping them in front of Daphne, he said loudly, "Here's some I thought you'd like, Daffy. *Make Way for Ducklings* and *The Story About Ping.*"

Everybody laughed except Mr. O'Brien, Daphne, and me. "Sit down and get to work, Tony," Mr. O'Brien said.

As I sat there reading *The Snowy Day,* I could hear everybody else laughing. They were reading funny things out loud and showing each other pictures they liked. At our table all I heard was the rustle of turning pages and an occasional sniff. I wanted to offer Daphne a Kleenex, but I didn't have any, so I gritted my teeth in frustration and tried to hear what was going on at Tracy's table.

They were all laughing at *In the Night Kitchen* because the little boy in the story is naked. It was a dumb thing to giggle at, but at least they were having fun.

"Look, Tony," Michelle shrieked. "Here's a picture of you!" She held up an illustration of Mickey falling into a milk bottle.

"Hey, that kid's indecent!" Tony snatched the book

away from Michelle and held it up for everyone to see. "Libraries shouldn't have dirty books like this lying around for little kids to see. Hey, Mr. O'Brien, look at this picture. The kid doesn't have any clothes on!"

Mr. O'Brien shrugged and reminded Tony that libraries are supposed to be quiet places. Then he came over to our table, which was, of course, a perfect little oasis of silence.

"How are you two doing?" He smiled down at us like a benevolent god, stroking his beard.

I shrugged, dropping my eyes to a picture of Peter discovering that snowballs melt. "Okay."

"Daphne?" He stared at the top of Daphne's head. Without looking up from an illustration of the ducklings parading across the street, Daphne mumbled something that sounded like "Fine."

"Have you gotten any ideas for your own book?" Mr. O'Brien sat down on a corner of the table.

When we both shook our heads, he looked at us, his face concerned. "Have you even talked about it?" He frowned when neither one of us answered. "You're supposed to have a plot outline ready next Monday and some sketches. Don't you think you better start talking?"

I felt my stomach tighten up. Never in all my life had I gotten a bad grade in English. Math, maybe. Even history or social studies. But never English. I looked at Daphne. She was still staring at the ducklings as if they were more real than either Mr. O'Brien or I was.

Sighing, Daphne closed the book. For a second, she looked at me with wide gray-green eyes, and then she looked past me at something behind my chair. Without thinking, I turned around to see what she was staring at now. In a glass display case was a collection of little mice like mine. Dressed in fine clothes, they were sitting on tiny chairs and sofas upholstered in red velvet. Their glass eyes sparkled as if they were enjoying the sight of Daphne and me peering into their cozy world.

"We could write a story about mice," I blurted out. As soon as I said it, I felt my face turn red. Compared to "The Nightmare Slumber Party," a story about mice sounded like something a six-year-old would write.

"That's a start," Mr. O'Brien said. "Real mice or toys like these?" He waved at the display case.

Still blushing, I told him that I had a collection of mice like the ones in the case. "One of them disappeared. Probably my cat dragged him off somewhere, but I was thinking the story could be about how the other mice look for him. It's supposed to be a children's book, isn't it?"

Mr. O'Brien nodded. "I think that sounds like a fine idea. What do you think, Daphne?"

Without looking at either one of us, she said it was okay with her.

Leaning toward her, I asked, "Can you draw mice like those?" I wanted her to look at me, I wanted her to answer me, so I stared at her, trying to force her to respond.

Briefly she glanced at me, her eyes meeting mine, and nodded. Then down went the head again, her hair tumbling between us.

Mr. O'Brien smiled encouragingly. "I can't wait to read it." Giving us each a little pat on the shoulder, he got up and walked to another table.

31

I finished looking at my stack of books and took them back to the cart. Catching Mom's eye, I walked over to the Adult Reading Room to say hello.

"That's quite a group you're with," Mom said. "Who's the rascal with the beautiful blond curls?"

"That's Tony Cisco. Isn't he awful?"

"I've had to send him back to the Children's Room twice. I keep finding him in the Periodical Room reading *Playboy*." Mom laughed. "I imagine he keeps Mr. O'Brien on his toes."

"Did you see Daphne?"

"No. Which one is she?"

"Over there, taking books off the cart. See her?"

Mom stared at Daphne for a few seconds. "Why, Jess, she's beautiful."

"Daphne?" I watched her carry her books back to our table, trying to see what Mom saw, but she looked the same as always to me. Tall and thin, her hair tangled by the wind, she sat alone, her pale face bent over an open book.

Puzzled, I shifted my gaze to Michelle, who was huddled at a table with Sherry and Tracy, giggling and whispering. If Mom had said that Michelle was beautiful, I wouldn't have been surprised. Her long blond hair fell in perfect waves over the shoulders of her lavender sweater, framing a face that boasted a short, straight nose, big blue eyes, and the kind of skin a pimple wouldn't dare disturb. Like the girls who appeared on the pages of *Seventeen*, Michelle always wore the right clothes and the right makeup, and she always exuded a sense of incredible self-confidence. She was

pretty, she knew she was pretty, and she knew everyone else knew it, too.

"You don't think so?" Mom asked.

I shook my head. "Daphne's too peculiar. Take
Michelle, for example." I pointed her out to Mom.
"She's the kind of girl everybody thinks is beautiful."

Mom looked at Michelle. "Too ordinary. No
character."

"How about Tracy and Sherry?"

"Cute," Mom said indifferently. "But nothing special."

"They're the most popular girls in our class."

Mom shrugged. "Daphne is unusual." She paused,
searching for the right words. "Delicate, ethereal, like a
princess in a tower waiting to be released from a spell."

I stole another glance at Daphne. Mom was right in
a way. There was something about her, something un-
common, something fragile. She had the look of a ballerina, slender and wide-eyed and proud.

"She reminds me of Arthur Rackham's illustrations," Mom mused. "The ones in that fairy tale book
you have at home. Those pale princesses with long,
dark, swirling hair."

I nodded, knowing now what Mom meant.

"Does she always look that sad?"

"Yes."

"I'd like to see her smile," Mom said. "I'd hate to
think she might really be as sad as she looks."

Before Mom could say anything else, she had to
rush off and help a woman find a travel guide to Hawaii.
Slowly I walked back to the table and sat down. I

wanted to say something to Daphne, but she didn't look up from *Where the Wild Things Are*. With a sigh, I opened a copy of *The Very Hungry Caterpillar*.

When it was time to go back to school, I stood up and pulled on my parka. Nervously, I glanced at Daphne, wondering if she thought I was going to walk with her, but she didn't even look at me. Grabbing her parka, she slipped away through the crowd of kids preparing themselves to leave the nice warm library and face the wind and the cold.

Relieved that I had gotten away from her so easily, I caught up with Tracy.

"Hey, Jess, you survived!" Michelle clapped me on the shoulder. "How was Ducky Daddles?"

I shrugged. "Not too bad. She hardly said a single word."

"Did you see that book *In the Night Kitchen*?" Sherry asked me.

"I have it at home," I said. "I got it for Christmas when I was little."

"Really? My mother wouldn't have let me *look* at a book like that." Sherry stared at me.

"Watch out, watch out, you'll be the last ones back to school and you'll get a spanking, just like Ping!" Tony ran past us and grabbed Michelle's comb out of her back pocket. Waving it over his head, he danced away from us backward, and we all ran after him, laughing and shouting, swerving around Daphne as she walked alone, her head down, her hands jammed into her pockets.

Five

 THE NEXT DAY, I walked to school with Tracy, Michelle, and Sherry. They were talking about a show they'd seen on television, one I'd missed because my mother doesn't allow me to watch horror movies.

"How about when she went in the kitchen and all the lights went out and she saw that guy with the knife in his hand?" Michelle blew a big bubble with her gum and popped it loudly. To my disappointment, it didn't even stick to her face.

"I screamed," Sherry said. "I was so scared. But you know what really grossed me out? When she was in the boat and that body floated up and its face was all eaten away."

Tracy shuddered. "Don't talk about it. I had nightmares so bad I woke up twice."

"Maybe we could put a scene like that in our book." Michelle popped her gum again.

"Well, I'm not going to draw a picture of it, that's for sure," Tracy said.

While they talked about the movie, I walked along shivering in the wind, trying not to feel sorry for myself. They were ignoring me because I hadn't seen the show, not because they didn't like me.

When we got to school, I went straight to my locker instead of following them into the girl's room. I'd had enough of them for a while. As I pulled out my books, I noticed Daphne a few feet away at her locker. Just as I was thinking about going over and saying hello to her, I saw Tony coming down the hall.

"Make way for ducklings, make way for ducklings!" he shouted, stepping around Daphne with exaggerated caution.

Swallowing hard, I walked down the hall, well behind Daphne. I certainly didn't want Tony to start teasing me.

When I sat down next to Daphne in English, I looked at her again, but she was already miles away, lost in a book, her hair hiding her face as usual.

Twisting my neck awkwardly, I saw the title of her book. *Green Mansions.* I'd never heard of it, and I wondered if it was a good story. Maybe I'd ask Mom to bring it home from the library.

After Mr. O'Brien had given us a lesson in transition, he told us to set up some sort of work schedule with our partners. "You should probably get together this weekend and decide on your story line. The illustrator could do some rough sketches. Then I could look them over on Monday and see if you're heading in the right direction."

Warily Daphne and I looked at each other. I had a feeling that she was just as reluctant as I was to spend any of our weekend together.

"Do you want to come over to my house on Saturday to look at the dollhouse and the mice?" I asked. "Or would Sunday be better?" I felt very awkward, and I was sure I sounded unfriendly.

Daphne shrugged, not bothering to look at me. "I don't care. Whichever's convenient for you." She spoke so softly I could barely hear her.

"Either day's okay with me." I tossed the choice back to her.

Somehow we agreed on Saturday afternoon, and I gave her my address. "Do you know where Willow Court is?"

She shook her head. "I don't know Adelphia very well."

"Where do you live?"

"On Cook's Lane."

"That's out in the country, isn't it?"

She nodded. "My grandmother has a farm."

"That's kind of far from where I live," I said. "How are you going to get to my house?"

Daphne shrugged. "I can walk."

"Walk? It must be two miles."

She shrugged again. "That's not far. Just draw me a map."

Opening my notebook, I bent over a piece of paper, glad to have a break in our conversation. Talking to Daphne was an exhausting experience. As I drew the map, I was acutely aware that Michelle and Tracy were watching me and giggling. Feeling very conscious of Michelle's eyes, I leaned toward Daphne.

"You can walk along this footpath," I said, "and cut across this field. Here's Willow Court, and this is my house." I made a little X in front of our townhouse. "It has a red door and green shutters and a big bush under the window. Do you think you can find it?"

"I guess so." She sounded a little unsure, but she took the map, folded it, and stuck it in her notebook.

Before I could say anything more, the bell rang. Daphne grabbed her books and scurried out the door without a backward glance, and I left more slowly.

After school, I met Tracy, Michelle, and Sherry on the footpath. Michelle turned to me, the wind whipping her hair around her face. "Are you going to Daffy's house tomorrow?"

"No, she's coming over here." I tried to sound as if I were really dreading her visit.

"Poor Jess." Tracy gave me a sympathetic pat on the arm.

"You should've gone to her house," Sherry said. "I'd love to know where she lives."

"She lives out on Cook's Lane," I said. "On a farm."

"I bet she lives in that old house near the Exxon station. You know the one I mean? The windows are all busted out and it's falling down, but people live in it." Michelle popped her gum. "Well, this is where me and Sherry leave you guys." She paused on the footbridge and looked at Tracy. "Call me tonight if you can go roller skating, Trace."

Grabbing Sherry's arm, Michelle ran across the bridge and up the path leading to Spice Wind Lane.

With the wind in our faces, Tracy and I scurried toward home. When we got to Tracy's turn-off, we paused. "Are you really going to Skateland?" I asked Tracy.

"If my mom will let me." She jiggled back and forth

from one foot to the other, trying to keep warm. "Do you want to come, too, Jess?" She looked a little embarrassed. "I was going to ask you, but you always say how much you hate going there."

"I thought you hated it, too." I stared at her, feeling betrayed.

She shrugged and looked away, obviously embarrassed. "Michelle and Sherry go every Friday night, and they say it's lots of fun. Practically everybody's there." She smiled a little uncertainly and brushed a flying strand of hair out of her eyes. "Come on and go, Jess. You'll have a great time."

I shook my head. "Not tonight. Maybe some other time, though." I tried to return her smile, but my mouth felt stiff. I couldn't imagine spending an evening at Skateland. For one thing, I could barely roller skate, and, for another, I was scared to death of the kind of kids who hung out there. Mean-looking boys who laughed if you fell down, tough girls in tight jeans who smoked in the girls' room and looked at you with hard eyes if you got in their way.

"Well, okay, I'll see you later, then. Good luck tomorrow with Daphne." Tracy hurried away toward her house, and I walked on, feeling very alone.

As I passed the tot lot, I remembered all the times that Tracy and I had played there, challenging each other to see who could swing highest, racing each other to the top of the jungle gym, daring each other to hang by our knees without holding on. Now the swings were empty and the wind was twirling them around, making a little sad song as it clinked their chains together.

Dumping my books on the ground, I sat down in a

swing and rocked slowly back and forth, listening to the wind moaning through the trees and thinking about Tracy.

She seemed a lot older all of a sudden. Today, for instance, I'd noticed that she was wearing eye shadow, something she had once vowed she would never do. And she'd gotten her ears pierced in November. Like Michelle and Sherry, she was spending more and more time going to the mall and talking about the cute boys she saw there.

I sighed and pumped harder, lifting the swing higher into the air. Clothes, makeup, and boys—was that all Tracy was interested in now? Letting the wind buffet the swing and sting my nose, I wondered why I wasn't interested in things like that. Were Tracy, Michelle, and Sherry stupid, boring people? Or was it me? Maybe there was something wrong with me. Maybe I was abnormal. Maybe, deep down inside, I was just as strange as Daphne.

A little frightened by my thoughts, I pumped with all my strength, sending the swing higher and higher. I wished that the chains would break and the wind would sweep me up, up, up into the sky, beyond the clouds, beyond the sun and the moon, to some marvelous kingdom where no one ever changed and friends were friends for life.

Six

AT THREE-THIRTY on Saturday afternoon, the doorbell rang, and there was Daphne, wearing her old red parka and a pair of baggy corduroy pants. Beside her stood a little girl. Her eyes, like Daphne's, were huge and green-gray, but her hair was blond and hung down her back in curly ripples. Despite her dirty, torn parka and her faded, outgrown jeans, she looked every bit as much like a princess as Daphne did.

"I'm sorry I'm late," Daphne mumbled, "but I had to bring Hope with me, and she can't walk very fast."

"That's okay." Ushering them inside, I shut the door against the arctic air. "You must be frozen," I said nervously. Now that Daphne was here, I had no idea what I was going to say to her.

"I feel like a snowman," Hope said. The wind had made her cheeks bloom with red and her eyes sparkled.

"Would you like some hot chocolate?" I asked.

Hope nodded. "I would love some."

Daphne looked uncomfortable. "If it's not too much trouble or anything."

They followed me into the kitchen and sat down at the table. Hope spotted Snuff lurking in a corner, watching the refrigerator hopefully.

"Is this your cat?" With a sudden lunge, Hope scooped up Snuff and buried her face in the cat's fur. "Oh, you pretty, pretty kitty, are you singing me a little song?"

"You better put her down," I said, recognizing Snuff's lovely growling song for what it was. "She's not very friendly."

"She wouldn't scratch me, would she?" Hope continued to cuddle Snuff against her body, but she looked a little uncertain.

"She might even bite you. She has a very nasty disposition."

"Oh." Looking very disappointed, Hope put Snuff down. "My grandmother has a lot of cats. Some of them are kind of wild and mean, but most of them are nice. Especially Callie. She's going to have kittens, and Grandmother says I can have one for my very own. Maybe you could have one, too, and then you'd have a nice kitty."

I smiled at Hope, glad that she was a lot more talkative than her sister. "That would be nice, Hope."

As I poured hot milk into our mugs, I glanced at Daphne. She was looking out the sliding glass door at the row of townhouses behind us. A wide strip of open space separated us from them, but they were close enough to see the people inside.

"Is the fat lady in the third one from the left doing

42

her yoga exercises?" I asked Daphne. Josh and I loved to watch her force herself into all sorts of strange contortions. We were sure that one day she'd get stuck and we'd have to call the rescue squad.

Daphne shook her head, killing that attempt to start a conversation.

"Do you have a mommy?" Hope asked suddenly.

I nodded. "She's at work today. She has to work every other Saturday at the library."

Hope nodded, looking relieved. "How about your daddy? Where's he?"

"He lives in California. He and Mom are divorced." I took a big sip of my hot chocolate and burned my tongue, something I do every single time I have hot chocolate.

"We don't have a daddy either. He went away a long time ago, before I was even born." Hope wiped her mouth, succeeding only in smudging her chocolate mustache. "Do you have any cookies?"

"Hope!" Daphne frowned, embarrassed, I guess, that Hope would ask me for food.

I laughed, trying to show Daphne she didn't need to be embarrassed. "Sure, if my brother hasn't eaten them all."

I rummaged around in the cupboard and found a bag of chocolate-chip cookies I'd hidden behind the Bran Buds. Knowing Josh never ate cereal, especially that kind, I'd figured the cookies might escape his notice.

"Where's your brother?" Hope asked, her mouth full of cookies. "Is he big or little?"

"He's big. Right now he's over at a friend's house."

43

She nodded and crammed a few more cookies into her mouth. I figured she could probably give Josh a run for the money as far as eating was concerned. Daphne, on the other hand, took one cookie and drank her hot chocolate slowly and deliberately, peering into the mug as if it were full of marvelous secrets.

After Hope and I finished the bag of cookies, I gathered up the mugs, rinsed them, and put them in the dishwasher. Then I led Daphne and Hope upstairs to my room.

"Is this your dollhouse?" Hope dropped to the floor and peered into each room, entranced by the mice and the furniture and the little chandeliers.

I turned to Daphne, who was staring down at the dollhouse, her pale face as expressionless as usual. "I wrote an outline for the story last night. Do you want to read it?"

As I handed it to her, I could feel my heart thudding. I realized then that I wanted Daphne to like my story. I wanted to impress her, I wanted her to realize that I wasn't just like all the other girls in our class.

While Hope investigated my shelf full of dolls and stuffed animals, Daphne sat down on the floor by the dollhouse and read my outline. When she finally looked up, she was frowning slightly. "It's very good except for the ending," she said uncertainly.

Disappointed, I stared at her. "What's wrong with the ending?"

"Well, I don't know. It sounds sort of funny to have the cat bring Sir Benjamin back." Nervously she ran her hand through her hair, smoothing it back from her face. "It seems kind of unrealistic."

44

"But I wanted it to have a happy ending." I felt my face flush with embarrassment.

Daphne twirled some of her hair around her finger and shrugged. "I think it would be better if it ended with Princess Heatherfern still looking for him. He hasn't come home, but she hasn't given up hoping."

I shrugged, not really agreeing with Daphne but not wanting to offend her. "Why don't we get started? You could make some sketches of the dollhouse and the mice."

Daphne opened her sketchbook and sat down cross-legged in front of the dollhouse. I could tell by the expression on her face that she was every bit as delighted with it as Hope had been.

As she began to sketch, I dropped down on the floor beside her and watched her long, slender fingers move across the paper. In a few seconds, the dollhouse began to emerge from sketchy pencil lines; first an outline of its shape, then its rooms, and finally its details.

"That's good," I whispered. "It looks just like it."

Daphne shook her head as if she didn't agree, but she looked at me. "It's such a beautiful dollhouse."

"I know. My grandfather made it for me when I was three years old. It was under the Christmas tree, and I don't think I even looked at any of the rest of my presents."

"I made Hope a dollhouse out of cardboard boxes, but it's so flimsy something breaks every time she plays with it."

"But it's a nice dollhouse anyway." Hope hugged Daphne. "It's like a castle with towers and everything, and she made me paper-doll princes and princesses.

45

There's even a unicorn for them to ride and a dragon for the princes to fight."

Daphne blushed and bent her head over her sketch book. She was drawing the mice now.

"My sister is the best artist in the world," Hope said proudly.

"She's wonderful," I agreed. "Look, you can even see their eyes sparkle." I pointed at the mice Daphne had drawn. "I wish I could draw like that."

Daphne looked embarrassed, but she smiled a little as if she were really pleased that I liked her drawings.

"Now," I said. "Let's put them in their rooms, the way they are at the beginning of the story." I picked up Princess Heatherfern and stood her in front of her window. "She's waiting for Benjamin."

Daphne moved Cragstar to the tower. "He's studying his books of magic, trying to find a spell that will show him where Benjamin is. But Malvolia is in the attic, plotting against him." Daphne moved Malvolia about, cackling to herself in a very witchy way.

"And what about Baby Mouse?" Hope picked him up. "What's he doing?"

"Hush, hush," I made Nurse Marigold say. "You must go to sleep, little one."

Hope looked disappointed. Instead of putting Baby Mouse in his cradle, she made him dance about the nursery, squeaking and singing a funny little song.

"My lady, my lady!" Daphne spoke gruffly for Cragstar as she moved him into Princess Heatherfern's room. "We must flee this house! Evil is afoot and danger lurks everywhere."

"But where shall we go? We cannot leave without Benjamin," I spoke in a quavery voice for the princess.

"We must seek Benjamin in the Enchanted Wood, for it is there that he has gone, led astray by the wiles of the wicked witch Malvolia." Daphne made Cragstar hop and skip about the tiny room.

I moved the princess closer to Cragstar. "I will brave the gravest dangers of the Enchanted Wood if you can lead me to Benjamin, venerable sir."

"But Malvolia enters the room!" Daphne flew Malvolia down from the attic. "You'll never find him, never! Hee, hee, hee!" Daphne cackled so hideously that Hope almost dropped Baby Mouse in alarm.

"Off with you, evil spirit!" Daphne-Cragstar roared, and we hustled the wizard and the princess past the witch and down the stairs.

"What about me?" squeaked Hope. "Can't I come too?"

"No, no, Hope," I said. "He's too little, and besides, that's not how the story goes." I made Nurse come scurrying after Baby Mouse.

"Now, you come back here, you bad baby, and get into your nice cradle!" I made the nurse say in a very stern voice.

But Hope's little hand stayed right where it was, and she looked up at me sadly. "He wants to come, Jessica."

I sighed, knowing I couldn't resist a look so full of longing. "Oh, all right. Have him hide in one of their supply baskets. Then he can hop out when they're too far away to go back."

Hope smiled, revealing two missing front teeth, and hopped Baby Mouse up and down. "I'm going, I'm going!" she squeaked.

Daphne and I smiled at each other over Hope's head. "Let's take them outside so they can have a real journey," Daphne suggested. "I could sketch their adventures more realistically that way."

Slowly we took the mice out of my room and down the stairs, a step at a time. In the kitchen they were in great peril from Snuff, but Cragstar brandished his staff bravely and chanted powerful anticat spells while the princess and the baby cowered under a chair.

Once the threat of Snuff was past, they raided the cupboards for supplies and escaped through the sliding glass door. Cautiously they made their way across the open space, in great danger of being carried away by birds, down a hill, and into a wooded gully. On the banks of the creek, we decided to build a shelter for them.

Gathering stones, we constructed a little house and roofed it with twigs and tufts of moss. By the time we were finished it was late in the afternoon, and Daphne's fingers were almost too cold to sketch the mice in front of their new home.

"Let's stop for today," I said. "My toes are about to freeze, and Hope's lips are turning blue." Gathering up the mice, I dropped them into my pocket.

"Shouldn't we leave them in their house?" Daphne asked.

"Something might happen to them out here." I thought of a cat or a dog knocking the little house apart, finding the mice, and taking them away. I'd already lost Benjamin. I didn't want to lose any of the others.

"They have a nice, snug house. They'll be safe," Daphne said.

Not wanting her to think I was being babyish, I reluctantly put the mice in their milkweed-pod beds. "Let's say they found this." Taking off one of my mittens, I covered all three with it. Then I put the roof back on and weighted it down with a few more stones. "There."

As we climbed up the hill toward home, I was surprised to see the moon hanging like a worn stone in the pale sky above the treetops. "It's almost dark," I said. "Do you want to stay and have dinner with us?"

Hope caught my hand and gave a little jump. "Could we?"

But Daphne shook her head. "No, thank you. We have to go home."

"Couldn't you call your mother and ask her?" I persisted.

"We don't have a phone."

I stared at Daphne, shocked. I thought everybody had a telephone. "My mother will drive you home, then. Come on, I'll ask her."

"Is she home now?" Hope asked.

I pointed at the lighted kitchen window in our house. "See her head? She's getting dinner ready." I looked at Daphne. "I really wish you could stay."

"No, we can't." Daphne tugged Hope away from me. "Come on, we have to hurry. We're late." All of a sudden the friendliness between us was gone, and

49

Daphne seemed as strange and unknowable as she did in school.

"Just stay right there, and I'll get my mom to drive you." Without waiting for a response, I ran into the house.

"Of course I'll take them home," Mom said. "It's much too cold and dark for them to walk way out there." She pulled on her coat and followed me outside.

Daphne and Hope were already a block away by the time we caught up with them, but Mom stopped and opened the door.

"Where are you going?" I asked Daphne. "I said we'd take you home."

"It's all right. I told you we could walk." Daphne stood there, pale in the harsh light of a street lamp.

Hope looked up at her. "Please, Daphne? I'm so cold, and I'm scared to walk in the dark."

"Come on, girls," Mom said kindly. "I need to pick up some milk at the store, so it's not a bit of trouble to drop you off." She leaned toward them, smiling, and Daphne finally opened the back door and got in, with Hope right behind her.

"Thank you very much," Daphne said softly. "I just didn't want you to go to any trouble."

"Don't worry about it," Mom said. "Just tell me how to get to your house."

Following Daphne's directions, Mom drove through Adelphia's curving streets and then out into the cold, dark farmland surrounding the town. To my relief, we passed the Exxon station without stopping. About two miles down Cook's Lane, Daphne pointed to a mailbox sagging open on a crooked post. "You can let us out right here," she said.

"It's dark, Daphne. I can't just drop you two by the side of the road. Is it up this driveway?" Mom slowed down to make the turn.

"Yes, but the house isn't far. We can walk easily."

Ignoring Daphne, Mom drove up a rutted driveway, bouncing us around when she hit the bumps. As we emerged from an arch of old trees, we saw a house standing all alone on a rise of ground, a tall, black shape against the starry sky. Not a light shone anywhere.

"Is anyone at home?" Mom sounded worried.

"She must be in the kitchen." Daphne opened the door, flooding the car with light. "Come on, Hope. She's probably worried to death."

"Thank you very much for bringing us home," Hope said. "And for letting Baby Mouse go on the journey," she added, smiling at me.

"Yes, thank you, Mrs. Taylor," Daphne said as she took Hope's hand. Together they ran across the yard and up the steps.

Mom sat there for a minute, staring at the house until she was sure they had gotten inside. Then she put the car in reverse and eased back down the driveway, hitting the bumps just as hard as she had coming in. Neither one of us said a word until we were back on Cook's Lane.

"Well, I hope everything was all right," Mom said. "That house looked so dark and lonely."

"I know." I shivered and moved a little closer to Mom. "I asked them to stay for dinner, but Daphne said they couldn't."

"It was nice of you to ask." Mom smiled at me. "How did it go today?"

I shrugged. "While we were working on the book, we had a great time. She was so different from the way she is in school. She talked and laughed, and she's a wonderful artist. I wish you could have seen the things she drew." I sighed. "But when they were leaving, she got all strange again. You saw how she was about the ride. Don't you think she acted kind of weird?"

"Oh, I don't know. I think she was uncomfortable about something. And shy." Mom paused. "And she's probably a little afraid to get too friendly with you, Jessica. After all, you haven't shown any interest in her before now, and she certainly doesn't have any reason to think that anyone at Oakcrest wants to be her friend."

"That's true." I leaned back against the car seat and thought about the afternoon I'd spent with Daphne and Hope. Strange as it seemed, I'd had the best time I'd had in a long time. In fact, I could hardly wait for Daphne to come over again. And not just to work on the book. There were so many things I didn't know about her, so many questions I wanted to ask her.

"Do you think maybe she likes me, then? Even if she did act funny about your giving her a ride home?" I asked Mom.

She smiled at me and patted my knee. "Of course she likes you. She wouldn't have stayed so long if she didn't." She slowed down to turn from Cook's Lane into Adelphia, leaving the bleak countryside behind. "Just be patient with her, Jess. Give her a little time. And don't let the kids at school make you forget that Daphne has feelings."

I stared at her, shocked. "I've never made fun of her, Mom! I wouldn't hurt her feelings for anything."

Seven

Unfortunately, it wasn't as easy for me to avoid hurting Daphne's feelings as I thought it would be. When I left for school on Monday, I told myself that I was going to be very friendly to Daphne and that I didn't care what Michelle said, did, or thought. Feeling proud of myself, I hurried down the hall to my locker, planning to walk right up to Daphne and say hello.

But just as I saw Daphne, Michelle and Tony stepped in between her and me. They were laughing and talking, and as Michelle's eye caught mine, I smiled at her and pretended not to see Daphne.

Stuffing my parka into my locker, I grabbed my books and hurried down the hall to walk with Tracy.

"Oh, Jess, you should've come to Skateland with us. I never had so much fun." Tracy grabbed my arm and giggled. "Scott asked me to skate couples with him twice, and Michelle asked him if he likes me and he said yes!" She hugged her books, her eyes shining. "Michelle thinks he's going to ask me to go with him."

"Really? That's neat, Tracy." I tried to smile at her, but it made me uncomfortable to see her acting more and more like Michelle. If she got a boyfriend, she'd never be my friend again. She would do everything with Michelle and Tony and Scott, and I would never see her.

Before I could say anything else, Michelle rushed up and butted in between Tracy and me. "Guess what Tony told me?" she asked Tracy.

While the two of them talked about Tony and Scott, I walked along, feeling forgotten. Ahead of me in the hall, I saw Daphne all by herself. I wanted to catch up with her, but I didn't have the courage. Instead, I trailed along with Tracy and Michelle, pretending to be interested in what had happened at Skateland.

In English, Mr. O'Brien gave us fifteen minutes to work on our books while he walked around the classroom looking at our outlines and sketches.

Mustering my courage, I tried to get Daphne's attention. She seemed as remote as always, as if Saturday had never happened. Finally she looked up at me.

"When can you come over again?" I asked her.

She shrugged. "Probably next Saturday." Without waiting for an answer, she bent her head over a drawing of Princess Heatherfern. "Look, Jessica," she said to the paper. "You don't have to be my friend just because we're doing this book together. I know you probably didn't want to be my partner, so you don't have to worry about hurting my feelings or anything."

I stared at her hair, falling like a curtain between us, and I wished I could see her face. It was hard to talk to hair.

"It's true," I whispered. "At first I was mad, but I don't feel like that anymore."

Daphne shrugged, making her shoulder blades jut out sharply under her faded black turtleneck. "You didn't seem very friendly this morning."

"When?" I felt my face flush as I remembered how I'd avoided her in the hall.

"At our lockers before school started."

"I didn't see you," I mumbled.

She looked at me then and caught me with a burning red face. "You saw me, Jessica. You just pretended not to."

It was my turn to look away, to stare at my desk and wish I had a long curtain of hair to draw across my face. "I did not pretend. I really didn't see you, Daphne," I muttered.

She sighed. "Well, I'll come over on Saturday so we can finish the story."

Then the bell rang, and she was up and gone before I had even picked up my books.

In the cafeteria I sat down next to Tracy. Daphne was sitting at the end of a table about three rows away, but her back was to me. After our conversation in English, I was too embarrassed to look at her, let alone go and sit beside her.

"Does my hair look funny?" Tracy asked me. "When I was curling it this morning, I just couldn't get the two sides to look the same." She lifted a strand to show me, then dropped it scowling.

"Then, when I was looking for my best jeans, I found them in the dirty-clothes basket, and somebody had thrown a wet towel on top of them. I was going to spray some perfume on them—I thought it would hide the moldy smell from the towel. But then I noticed they had a big spot on the knee like I'd spilled ketchup on them or something, so I had to wear these, and they don't fit me nearly as well." Tracy plucked at her jeans. "Do they look too terrible, Jess?"

I shook my head, wishing I could think of a way to make her talk about something more interesting than her jeans and her hair.

I didn't have to worry long. Michelle and Sherry came over, and Michelle plopped her tray down next to Tracy. Leaning toward me, she said, "You and Daffy looked real friendly in English today."

Embarrassed, I stared down at my sandwich. "We were just talking about our book," I said. I wanted to say more, I wanted to tell them how different Daphne had been from her usual school self, but I knew they wouldn't understand. Somehow they'd turn it all around and start laughing at me.

"What was she like?" Sherry asked.

I saw her nudge Michelle, and I knew Michelle was trying not to laugh. "Yes, Jessica, tell us all about your Saturday with Daffy Duck," Michelle said, pretending to be very serious.

I shrugged. "I showed her the story and she started drawing the pictures. She's really a good artist."

"Is it about ducks?" Sherry asked, trying to keep her face straight.

"No, it's about mice." Somehow I knew they were going to think that was funny.

"Mice?" Sherry and Michelle started laughing. "Your story is about mice?"

Just as Sherry and Michelle were about to have hysterics, Tony, Scott, and Mike sat down at our table. Luckily for me, they forgot all about Daphne and me and concentrated their attention on the boys. Tracy, though, did give me a sympathetic look before she started teasing Scott about something he'd said to her before school.

For the rest of the week Daphne ignored me, and so did everyone else. Tracy, Michelle, and Sherry spent most of their time giggling and following Tony, Scott, and Mike up and down the halls. I was so unhappy that I had to force myself to get up and go to school, but I tried to act as if nothing was wrong. I was sure that if I let Michelle know that she was hurting my feelings, she would do worse things than pass notes like the one I saw in Science.

She had written the note to Sherry. After Sherry read it and giggled, she left it lying on her desk. Since I sat next to her, it was easy for me to see it.

"Once upon a time, Jessica Mouse built a little house," I read. Michelle had illustrated it with a crudely drawn mouse wearing glasses.

Unhappily, I stared at my textbook, trying to read the paragraph Mrs. Kaufmann was talking about, but the words blurred. They thought I was a baby, a mouse, a little nothing. Could I help being short and skinny? Could I help wearing glasses? It just wasn't fair. Nothing was fair.

Glancing across the room, I saw Daphne, half-turned away, gazing out the window at the wintry sky and bare trees. Before I could look away, she stared back at me for a second, her eyes catching mine. Then, tossing her hair, she turned back to the window.

On Saturday, I lounged around the house, afraid to go anywhere in case Daphne came to see me. She hadn't said another word about doing any more work on the story, but I hoped she would show up.

At two o'clock, the doorbell rang. Daphne and Hope stood on the steps, shivering in the cold cold air.

"It's mice time!" Hope said, hopping up and down. "Squeak, squeak, Jessica!"

I laughed and invited them in for hot cocoa. This time, Mom was home, and she served us all some brownies we'd made earlier in the morning. That pleased Hope very much.

"Where do you put them all?" Mom asked Hope as she finished her fourth one.

"Right here!" Hope rubbed her tummy and laughed. She liked my mother a lot, but Daphne seemed as suspicious of Mom as she was of everybody. No matter how hard Mom tried to get a conversation going, Daphne sat silent as a statue, slowly eating one brownie and sipping her cocoa as if she were afraid of burning her tongue.

"Do you want to work on the story now?" Daphne asked. It was almost the first thing she'd said since she'd sat down at the kitchen table.

"Sure." We rinsed our cups and plates, grabbed our jackets, and ran outside.

As soon as we spotted the mouse house, I knew everything was all right. The roof was intact and, as

59

soon as we took it off, I saw the three mice, still sleeping safely under my mitten.

The creek was frozen near the banks, but we built a raft and let the mice sail down the middle, past ice grottoes where Frost Giants tried to catch them, between cliffs where trolls hurled boulders down at them, and finally to a safe landing on a pebbly strip of beach near a footbridge.

Once they were safely ashore, we built a new house for them. While the princess and the wizard rested, Hope and Baby Mouse went off to explore the forest.

"Do you still think the story should have an unhappy ending?" I asked Daphne.

She looked up from her sketch book. "Have you found Sir Benjamin in real life?"

I shook my head sadly. "Not a sign of him."

"Well, then, I don't think Princess Heatherfern should find him in the story. Sometimes people really do go away and you never see them again. Never." She shook her head, but she didn't look at me.

It bothered me the way she repeated "never." Her face looked so unhappy and her voice sounded as cold and dull as the winter wind sighing through the branches overhead.

"But this is a magical story," I said. "It doesn't have to be like real life. In stories you can make things come out the way you want them to."

Daphne shook her head. "Sir Benjamin is gone for good, and Princess Heatherfern has to accept that."

A gust of wind found its way down the back of my

neck and I shivered. "Maybe you should write the story." Even to me, my voice sounded nasty. Babyish.

Daphne looked at me then. "I'm sorry, Jessica. It's your story. End it any way you please." Closing her sketch book, she got up.

"Where are you going? You haven't finished the drawings yet, have you?" I scrambled up, too.

She shrugged. "I don't want to be so late getting home this time. Just tell me how you want to end the story, and I can draw a few more pictures before I go."

I picked up Princess Heatherfern and stared at her bright little eyes. "Well, suppose she's standing here on this rock." Kneeling down, I stood the little mouse on a rock. "And she's looking down the river and wondering if she'll ever see Sir Benjamin again. Then Cragstar could climb up next to her." I looked at Daphne, silently entreating her to pick up the wizard and start the story going again. Without her help, I knew I couldn't finish the book.

Solemnly, Daphne placed the wizard next to the princess. "Ah, my lady," she said in her deep wizard voice. "Another day has passed and there is still no sign of him. You must accept the sad truth that he is gone forever. You will never see him more. Never, my lady, never."

At each "never" I winced, but I turned the princess toward Cragstar and said in a very brave voice, "But we will keep looking, Cragstar. We will never give up hoping."

Daphne shook her head, but whatever she was

about to say was interrupted by a voice above us on the footbridge.

"What on earth are you doing, Jess?" Tracy was staring at Daphne and me.

"They're playing mice!" Michelle shrieked with laughter.

"We are not!" I sprang to my feet, lost my balance, and stepped into the icy creek. Yanking my soaked shoe out of the water, I glared at Tracy and Michelle. "We're writing our story!"

"Oh, sure." Michelle rolled her ten-speed bike along the bridge, still laughing. "Jessica Mouse, that's you. Why don't you grow up, little girl?"

Tracy frowned at Michelle. "They're just doing it so Daphne can draw them better."

Michelle laughed again. "Quack, quack, make way for ducklings!" Shoving off with one foot, she pedaled up the path, still laughing, and Tracy followed her, giving me one vexed look before she disappeared.

In the sudden silence, Daphne and I stared at each other. Nervously I shoved my glasses back up on my nose. Picking up Princess Heatherfern, I moved her to the edge of the rock. "Good-bye, cruel world," I said in a sad little voice and pretended I was going to drop her in the creek.

"No, no, my lady!" Daphne moved Cragstar in front of the princess. "We must never give up hope, remember?"

At that, I started to laugh and so did Daphne. My wet shoe, the expression on Tracy's face, the dumb little pink hat Michelle had been wearing, all seemed so funny that we laughed harder and harder.

"What's so funny? Why are you laughing?" Hope came running out of the woods. "Tell me, tell me!"

But neither of us could stop laughing long enough to tell her. Finally Daphne pulled herself together. "Where have you been, Hope?"

"At the tot lot. Baby Mouse had lots of adventures there." Hope capered about, laughing and singing a little song about Baby Mouse.

"Come on." Daphne swung Hope up and gave her a hug. "We have to go home."

"No, I don't want to." Hope squirmed and tried to get down. "I want to stay here and have some more adventures with the mice."

"No, no, we have to go, Hope." Daphne was insistent. "Remember how upset Grandmother was last week?"

"I'm tired," Hope said, sticking out her lip.

"Mom could give you a ride," I said.

"No, we can walk. Come on, Hopesy-Dopesy, I'll carry you piggyback." Daphne slung Hope around and settled her on her back. "Let's go!"

"Giddyup, horsey!" Hope shouted.

As they started galloping up the path, I called after them. "Are you coming back?"

But Daphne didn't answer. The wind was blowing harder, and Hope was still yelling "Giddyup!" Maybe she didn't hear me.

Stuffing the mice into my pocket, I jumped over the creek and ran across the open space, suddenly aware of how cold and wet my foot was.

"Where are Daphne and Hope?" Mom asked when I came in through the sliding door.

"They went home."

"I would have gladly given them a ride." Mom peered outside at the wintry dusk. "It's so cold out there. And it's such a long way. Do you think we should get the car and go after them?"

I shook my head. "I think it would make Daphne mad."

Mom sighed. "You're probably right." She looked at me. "Is Daphne always that quiet?"

"Not when we're playing the mice game." I blushed, realizing what I'd just said. "Not playing. I mean working out our story."

"She's a strange one." Mom turned to the stove and stirred something that smelled delicious. "Does she live with her parents or what?"

"Hope said their father went away, and they've never said anything about their mother. As far as I can tell, they live with their grandmother." I gave Mom a hug. "I think something sad has happened in their lives."

"Daphne does look unhappy." Mom gave me a nice warm hug in return. "Maybe their parents got a divorce and somehow the kids ended up with their grandmother. That happens a lot."

"Do you think stories should have happy endings or unhappy endings?" I asked Mom.

She looked a little surprised by my question, but she gave it some thought before answering. "I guess it depends on the story, honey. You wouldn't want to put a happy ending on if it would make the story seem false. The ending should be natural." She smiled at me. "Are you worrying about your Write-a-Book story?"

I nodded. "Daphne doesn't think the mice should find Sir Benjamin, but I kind of wanted them to. We compromised, though. They don't find him, but they promise to keep on looking for him. Do you think that sounds like a good ending?"

Mom nodded. "I hope you'll let me read it when you and Daphne are finished." She opened the refrigerator. "Want to fix a salad, Jess?"

"Sure." While I was chopping up a cucumber, I heard the front door slam.

"Hi, everybody. When are we eating?" Josh bellowed from the hall. "I'm starving."

Loping into the kitchen, Josh poked around in the salad bowl and grabbed a wedge of tomato.

"Hey, keep out of that! It's for dinner!" I shouted at him.

Turning to Mom, he picked up a spoon and stirred the contents of the frying pan. "What's all this junk on the chicken? Can't we ever have just plain old-fashioned fried chicken?"

Mom swatted him on the seat of the pants with the spatula. "It's tomato sauce and green peppers," she said. "Now go get cleaned up. Ed will be here in fifteen minutes."

"Is he eating here again tonight? He was just here last week. Can't he cook his own meals?" Josh scowled. "I thought you were so liberated, and here you are, cooking up all this fancy stuff with tomato sauce all over it."

"That's enough, Josh!" Mom's face reddened, and I thought she was going to use the spatula in earnest on Josh's rear end.

65

Mumbling something else about tomato sauce, Josh poured himself a glass of milk and disappeared into the living room.

Mom sent me a questioning look, but I returned my attention to the cucumber. Slicing it as thin as possible, I avoided looking at Mom. Secretly I agreed with Josh about Ed, but I didn't want to start a family argument by saying so.

Not that there was anything wrong with Ed. He was nice, and for a man his age, he was still pretty good-looking. But having him around every weekend upset the balance in our house. He took too much of Mom's attention, for one thing, and for another, he made her act silly, like a teenager.

While I was tossing the salad, the doorbell rang, and Mom scurried down the hall to let Ed in. She was patting her hair and tugging at her jeans as if she were Tracy on the way to meet Scott instead of a middle-aged mother. Embarrassed, I glanced at Josh. He rolled his eyes up to the ceiling and groaned.

"Hi, Jessie!" Ed bounded into the kitchen, all smiles, a bottle of wine in one hand and a half-gallon of chocolate-chip ice cream in the other. "Hi, Josh!"

We both smiled politely, and Josh caught the ice cream when Ed tossed it to him. Putting it in the freezer, Josh folded his arms, leaned back against the refrigerator door, and tried to look sulky.

"Boy, oh, boy, something sure smells good!" Giving me a wink, Ed followed Mom to the stove. "What does my favorite French chef have on the menu tonight?"

Mom flashed Ed a smile that Tracy would have envied. "*Italiano, signore.* Chicken cacciatore."

Ed gave Mom a kiss and hovered over the stove, lifting lids, stirring, sniffing, tasting. If he had been Josh, he would have gotten his fingers whacked more than once, but Mom just smiled and watched him.

"Wonderful, wonderful!" Ed smacked his lips and kissed Mom again. "My Italian grandmother couldn't have cooked up a better meal than this." Smiling at Josh and me, he gave us both a taste of the sauce.

By the time we sat down at the table, everybody was in a good mood. Ed told us funny stories about his Italian grandmother, which Mom matched with stories about her Irish grandfather. We laughed so hard we could hardly eat, but somehow we managed to finish everything, even the ice cream.

After dinner, we all cleaned up the kitchen. Ed even mopped the floor while singing an aria from *The Barber of Seville*. Just to keep us in a nice Italian mood, he said.

"How about playing a game of Clue?" Ed asked as Josh and I plopped down on the couch to watch television.

To my surprise, Josh agreed without even putting up an argument. We played four games, and I actually won once. Josh, of course, won twice, and Mom won the last game. Poor Ed lost every time.

Around eleven, Josh and I went upstairs. In the hall outside the bathroom door, I smiled at Josh.

"He's really not so bad, is he?"

Josh shrugged. "He could be worse."

"Well, he doesn't sing very well, and he's a terrible Clue player, but he's funny."

"Yeah, I guess so." Josh scratched his head. "And I have to admit, we eat better when he's around. Even that tomato sauce turned out to be good." With that, he gave me a shove and ducked into the bathroom, slamming the door shut behind him

"Hey!" I shouted, "I was going in there!"

"Tough luck, Jess-o!" Josh yelled back.

Eight

I SPENT practically all of Sunday shut up in my room working on "The Mysterious Disappearance of Sir Benjamin Mouse." When it was finally typed, the sky outside my window was flushed red with a winter sunset. My back ached, my fingers were sore, and I was very tired, but I felt like a real writer.

I looked at the stack of paper on my desk. Eight pages I'd typed. Eight. I'd never written anything that long before. And it had an ending, something most of my earlier stories had lacked. I'd lost interest in them and they'd just stopped, sometimes in the middle of a sentence.

But this one had a real ending. Not the sappy "and they lived happily ever after" ending I'd planned to give it. Daphne had been right. I would have ruined the story if it hadn't been for her advice.

I stretched and got up, eager to go to school and show it to her. I hoped she would like it.

As I hurried along the footpath Monday morning, I

wondered if Daphne had finished any of the illustrations. They weren't due until Friday, but I was eager to see them.

Although I looked for Daphne by her locker, I didn't see her. Unfortunately, I did see Michelle.

"Hi, Jessie," Michelle smirked at me, showing her little white teeth in a nasty grin. "How are the mice?"

"Squeak, squeak," Sherry whispered, jostling against me from the other side.

Before I could say anything, the two of them ran off down the hall. Gritting my teeth, I walked along behind them, hating them both so much I ached.

When I got to English, I stared at Daphne's empty desk in surprise. Where was she? She'd never been absent before. Anxiously I glanced around the room, but I didn't see her anywhere. Disappointed, I got out my notebook and tried to pay attention to what Mr. O'Brien had to say about transitions.

Although I was sure Daphne would be in school Tuesday, she wasn't there. Nor was she there on Wednesday. On Thursday she was still absent, but I had an early dismissal that day because of an appointment with my orthodontist. After Dr. West had finished tightening my braces, I asked Mom if we could drive past Daphne's house.

"Maybe I could just drop in and see if she's coming to school tomorrow. Or if she's finished the illustrations, I could take them to Mr. O'Brien for her."

Mom nodded and drove out of Adelphia, leaving behind all the curving streets and cul-de-sacs lined with look-alike houses and townhouses and apartments. Out in the country, everything was bare and brown and shaggy, unplanned and natural. Farmhouses and bungalows sprang up here and there as if they'd grown out of the earth all by themselves.

As Mom rounded a curve, I saw three people walking along the side of the road, their backs to us. One was an old lady wearing a man's red plaid lumber jacket and a fur hat. Her tall, thin body was hunched over a grocery cart full of trash. The other two, pulling bottles and cans out of the tangled grass and bushes and loading them into the cart, were Daphne and Hope.

Shocked, I slid down in the seat. "Don't stop, Mom! Just drive right past like you don't even see them!"

I guess Mom must have been just as surprised as I was because she did exactly what I told her to do. As soon as we were safely around a bend in the road, I sat up and stared at Mom.

"How come Daphne was outside?" I asked. "If she's well enough to walk along the road like that, she should be in school."

Mom shook her head. "I don't know, Jess. I would have stopped, but I was afraid of embarrassing them."

"What were they doing?"

"Collecting bottles and cans. They're probably going to return them to the store for money."

"Do you think they're that poor?"

"I hope not, honey." Mom didn't sound very sure.

"I guess that was their grandmother." I shuddered. No wonder Daphne had been worried about upsetting her. Even from the back, she'd looked kind of strange and scary.

We rode the rest of the way home in silence. As we turned into our court, I said, "I hope Daphne comes back to school tomorrow. Our stories are due, and I don't want to get a bad mark in English."

But Daphne didn't come to school on Friday, and I had to turn in my story without any pictures.

After class, Mr. O'Brien took me aside. "I know you're upset, Jessica, but people can't help getting sick. Don't worry. I won't lower your grade because Daphne isn't here to give me the illustrations."

I nodded. It was a relief to know that I wasn't going to get an E because of Daphne.

"Have you talked to her?" Mr. O'Brien asked.

"She doesn't have a phone."

Mr. O'Brien raised his eyebrows. "Do you know where she lives?"

"My mother drove her home once. Her house is way out Cook's Lane." I hesitated. "Do you want me to go out there and see what's wrong with her?"

Mr. O'Brien smiled at me. "That would be a wonderful thing to do, Jessica. I'd go myself, but I don't have much free time. Could you go tomorrow?"

I nodded my head and tried to smile back, but I was a little uneasy. It was a long walk, and even though I was curious, I was worried about having to meet Daphne's grandmother. I had a feeling that she wasn't a very friendly person.

It was very cold on Saturday. Since Mom was working, I had to walk, and if I hadn't promised Mr. O'Brien that I would go, I'd probably have turned around and gone home before I was halfway there.

When I got to the mailbox at the end of the drive, I hesitated. A line of trees hid the house from the road, making it impossible to tell whether anyone was home.

Suppose Daphne wasn't there? Reminding myself for the hundredth time that I'd promised Mr. O'Brien, I shoved my cold hands into my pockets and trudged slowly up the driveway. Above my head, the wind rocked the branches of the trees and hissed through the weeds in the fields on either side of me.

The house finally came into sight. It was old, Victorian, I guess, and quite a bit larger than I'd thought. It sported a tower, dormers, several stained-glass windows, and enough fancy trim to have kept a woodworker employed for years. Two enormous oak trees, heavily draped with ivy, flanked it like guardians, but the lawn surrounding it had long since gone to weed.

Never had I seen a sadder, more desolate house. The paint was flaking and peeling away, exposing the bare wood to the wind and the rain. Many shutters were missing, and those that remained hung crooked, their slats broken. The roof over the front porch sagged, railings had pulled away, much of the gingerbread was cracked. If I hadn't known better, I would have thought that the house had been vacant for years.

Crossing the yard quickly, I ran up the steps and knocked softly on the front door. At the sound, several cats emerged from the bushes around the house. Meowing hopefully, they rubbed against my legs and looked at the closed door. They were so thin I could feel their backbones when I petted them.

The cats and I stood there waiting, but there wasn't a sound in the house. Nervously I knocked a little harder. Still nothing.

Two narrow, small-paned windows flanked the door, and I pressed my face against one, trying to see inside. Through the grime, I could make out an empty hallway and a flight of stairs. Bundles of newspaper lined one wall, and shopping bags and boxes full of bottles and cans were stacked on the steps.

The cats meowed louder. There must have been a dozen of them milling around my legs, purring and mewing. Once more I raised my hand to knock, but before my fist hit the wood, the door opened and I almost hit Daphne instead.

She jumped back, obviously surprised, and I thought I was doing to die of embarrassment.

"I'm sorry, I was about to knock." I stood there, my face crimson.

Daphne stared at me for a minute, and then she started to laugh. Realizing how foolish I must have looked, I started to laugh, too. We both leaned against the wall, laughing till tears ran down our faces.

"Daphne, who's at the door? Who's there?" A voice rang out sharply from somewhere in the house, scaring me out of my giggles. "If it's somebody selling something, you tell them we don't want any!"

"It's all right, Grandmother," Daphne called. "It's just somebody from school." Turning back to me, Daphne was her usual somber self. "What are you doing here?"

A little bewildered by the sudden change in her, I told her I'd come to see if she'd finished the pictures for our book. "They were due yesterday, and Mr. O'Brien was worried about you. He asked me to come out here." Now that she was acting so cold, I certainly wasn't going to tell her that it had been my idea.

"Wait here. I'll get them for you." Shutting the door

in my face, she left me alone on the porch. The cats had dashed inside the second the door opened.

I felt like turning around and going home, but I hesitated, not wanting to leave without the pictures. Then a movement at one of the windows caught my eye. Through the glass I saw Hope, smiling and waving at me.

Yanking the door open, she stuck her head out. "Hi, Jessica! Did you walk all the way out here?"

I nodded and smiled at her, reminding myself that it was her rude sister, not Hope, that I was mad at.

"Is that door open?" The old woman I'd seen on the road stepped into the hall behind Hope. Seeing me, she frowned. "Who are you?"

"This is Jessica," Hope said. "She goes to Daphne's school." Seizing my hand, Hope pulled me into the house, letting the door slam shut.

I looked at their grandmother apprehensively. "Daphne went upstairs to get something for me," I said.

The old woman didn't look at all pleased to have company. She stared at me out of sunken, red-rimmed eyes. Her mouth twitched and she rubbed one hand against the other, making a dry rustly noise.

"You're from Adelphia, aren't you?" The woman stepped a little closer, her sharp old eyes taking in every detail of my appearance.

I nodded and glanced toward the stairs, wishing Daphne would come back. I wanted to go home, I wanted to get away from Daphne's grandmother. I didn't like the house; it was dark and cold, full of trash and stinking of cats. But I was too scared to move.

"You've got that Adelphia look," the old woman

75

went on. "Everybody there looks the same. Little cardboard houses popping up everywhere, everybody driving those cheap little cars, throwing their trash all over the place." She glared at me, her hands rubbing together faster and faster. "You won't see me selling my land to any fast-talking developer. I won't have any of those flimsy things on my farm. You hear?"

I looked desperately at Hope, but she just stood there, twirling her hair around one of her fingers and gazing out the window. I wanted to tell her to go get Daphne, but I was afraid her grandmother would become even more agitated.

"What's the matter with you, girl? Haven't you got anything to say for yourself?" The old woman shoved her face so close to mine that I could see the pores in her skin.

"Here are the pictures." Daphne thumped down the stairs and thrust a brown envelope at me. Turning to her grandmother, she said, "This is Jessica Taylor."

The old woman nodded. "She's from Adelphia."

"Jessica, this is my grandmother, Mrs. Woodleigh." Daphne grabbed her parka from a coat tree in the corner. "Come on," she said to me. "I'll walk down the drive with you."

Reaching for her jacket, Hope said, "I want to come, too."

Mrs. Woodleigh grabbed her arm. "No, no, it's too cold outside for my baby. You stay here with Granny."

The door thunked shut, cutting off a disappointed cry from Hope. Daphne hurried down the steps ahead of me, her hair billowing in the wind, and I ran after her, glad to breathe in the fresh, cold air.

When we reached the driveway, Daphne slowed down to a walk and I caught up with her. "Are you coming back to school Monday?"

She glanced at me, then gazed off into the distance, where the houses of Adelphia seemed to be marching over the hills toward Mrs. Woodleigh's farm. "I don't think so," she said, her face hidden.

"You don't seem sick." I stared at her. "What's wrong with you?"

She shrugged. "I don't know. I think I probably have mononucleosis."

"What's that? Is it contagious?"

"Only if you drink out of a glass I drank out of." She turned toward me then, her face worried. "Will you tell Mr. O'Brien that I have mononucleosis?"

"Sure." I said it over a few times in my mind, so I'd be sure to remember it. "When will you be back?"

"Not for a long time. It takes months to get over it."

"But what about your schoolwork? How will you make it all up?" I stared at her, puzzled by her lack of concern. I couldn't imagine being that nonchalant about missing so much school. "Do you want me to bring you your assignments?"

Daphne turned to me, surprised. "I couldn't ask you to do that, Jessica. No, that's okay." She looked down at the ground, nudging the ice on a puddle with her toe until it broke with a little tinkling sound.

"You're not asking me to do it, Daphne. I'm offering." I smiled at her uncertainly. "I don't mind. Honest, I don't."

Daphne brushed her hair back from her face and smiled at me. "You really wouldn't mind?"

I shook my head. "It's okay."

"That's awfully nice of you, Jessica." Daphne's eyes probed mine, as if she weren't quite sure she could trust me.

"Will your grandmother mind if I come out to see you?" I remembered Mrs. Woodleigh's scowling face. "I don't think she likes me very much."

Daphne sighed. "Grandmother is awfully suspicious of strangers. That's why I didn't invite you in. I knew she'd act like that. I thought if you saw her, you'd never come back." Daphne laughed uneasily. "It takes a while to get used to Grandmother."

"Do you and Hope live alone with her?"

Daphne nodded. "Our father was killed in Vietnam before Hope was born," she said slowly. "I don't remember him very well. I was only five when he died."

I waited for her to go on, to say something about her mother, but Daphne was silent. Her hair had blown back across her face, but I knew how unhappy she must feel. Aching with the frustration of not knowing what to say, I clutched the envelope she'd given me.

When the wind rattled the envelope, Daphne looked at me. "I hope you like the pictures I drew."

"Can I look at them now?"

"If you want. Come on, I'll take you to a place where we can get out of the wind." Running ahead of me, she led me behind the house to a grove of tall birches, their trunks silvery in the sunlight. She sat down on the trunk of a fallen tree and beckoned me to join her.

Opening the envelope, I pulled out eight pictures, one for each page, plus a title page and a jacket. Each picture was painted in muted colors, delicately drawn and filled with detail. Not another book in our class had illustrations like these.

"They're beautiful," I sighed, loving each one. "You're a real artist, Daphne."

"Do you really like them?" She looked pleased. "Is Sir Benjamin's hat right? I was a little worried about the plume."

"It's perfect." I smiled at her and put the drawings carefully into the envelope. "I can't wait to show them to Mr. O'Brien."

Daphne smiled again. "I loved drawing them. And making up the story. Hope still talks about Baby Mouse."

"Maybe we could write a sequel," I said. "When I bring you your homework next week, I could bring the mice along with me."

"That's a wonderful idea, Jessica." Daphne sprang to her feet and walked up the tree trunk, balancing with her arms outspread as the trunk got narrower. Laughing, I followed her and we climbed up into the branches and sat there, letting the wind rock us.

"Way out here, we won't have to worry about Michelle coming along and spoiling things," I said.

"I thought you were friends with her," Daphne said.

I shook my head. "I hate Michelle. And Sherry too."

"But you eat lunch with them and you walk around with them." Daphne looked puzzled.

"Only because I like Tracy. She's nice."

"I hadn't noticed," Daphne said quietly.

I looked up at her sharply. "Tracy's not really like Michelle and Sherry," I said defensively. "We've been best friends since we were in kindergarten, but now, I don't know. . . ." My voice trailed away. "She's changed, I guess."

Daphne nodded, but she didn't say anything.

"I'm sorry they've been mean to you," I finally said.

Daphne shrugged. "I don't want to talk about it."

Embarrassed at the unhappiness in Daphne's voice, I sat quietly on my branch, listening to the wind moan in the treetops. Faintly I heard a voice calling Daphne. Looking toward the house, I saw Mrs. Woodleigh on the back porch. From this far away, she was no taller than my finger.

"I guess I better go," Daphne said. "Grandmother worries about me if I'm gone too long." She climbed down from the tree, and I followed her.

"Would you like to come inside and have a cup of tea?" Daphne asked.

"Will your grandmother mind?"

"It'll be all right. She's just old. Once she gets to know you, she'll be nicer."

I was afraid I would hurt Daphne's feelings if I refused, so I smiled and walked across the yard with her. I hoped she couldn't hear my heart thumping. It seemed awfully loud to me.

Mrs. Woodleigh frowned at me as I climbed the back steps. "I thought you went home."

"Jessica's going to have a cup of tea before she goes, Grandmother," Daphne said. "It's a long, cold walk."

The kitchen was large and sunny, high-ceilinged

and warm, but like the rest of the house, it had been neglected for years. The walls were stained with grease and smoke, the corners were thick with cobwebs, and the paint was peeling. Like the hall, it stank of cats and garbage.

"Would you like a cup, Grandmother?" Daphne asked as she filled the kettle.

Mrs. Woodleigh lowered herself stiffly into a chair. "I suppose so, if you can make it the way I like it. Nice and hot and not too strong."

"Can I have some, too?" Hope asked as Daphne got cups out of a cabinet over the sink.

"Of course."

While Daphne busied herself making tea, I gazed around the room, trying to avoid looking at Mrs. Woodleigh. As my eyes traveled up the walls to the ceiling, she leaned toward me and grabbed my arm.

"You're worried about that, aren't you?" She pointed at a crack running up one wall and across the ceiling. "The house is going to collapse soon. It'll start right there and then the whole place will come down on our heads. Buried alive, buried alive, that's what we'll be."

Hope, who had been leaning silently against her grandmother, pulled away, her face frightened.

"You know that's not true, Grandmother." Daphne gave Hope a reassuring hug. "The whole house isn't going to fall down because of one little crack."

Mrs. Woodleigh shook her head and pursed her mouth into a tight little frown. She knew better, she did. Taking the cup Daphne offered her, she blew on the tea and took a noisy sip. With a shaky hand she slammed the cup down. "There's too much sugar in it! Can't you ever learn to fix it the way I like it?"

Daphne sighed. "I put one teaspoon in, Grandmother, just like you told me to."

Mrs. Woodleigh glared at Daphne. "You may think I'm a foolish old lady, but I know what's going on."

"Would you like me to fix you another cup? You could put the sugar in yourself this time." Daphne stared at her grandmother, her pale face expressionless.

"No, I don't want any now." The old woman pushed the cup away and frowned at me as if it were all my fault. "This house is going to ruin. Just like the whole country. Nothing is any good anymore."

I toyed with my teacup, turning it round and round on its saucer. I didn't know what to say.

"If they would just let John come home, everything would be all right," Mrs. Woodleigh said. "He'd take care of us, he'd fix the crack, he'd keep the house from falling down on us, wouldn't he?" She looked at Daphne, her face filled with anxiety. "How long are they going to keep him in that place? Why won't they let him leave Vietnam?"

Daphne touched her grandmother's shoulder gently. "Would you like to take your nap now?" she asked.

"I just don't know how much longer I can wait. It's not right for them to keep him there, not when we need him so bad." Rubbing her hands together, Mrs. Woodleigh got up and allowed Daphne to lead her out of the room. At the doorway, she paused and looked at the crack. "It won't be long now, will it?"

82

As Mrs. Woodleigh shuffled up the stairs, I turned to Hope. My heart was thumping hard again. "Was she talking about your father?" I whispered.

Hope nodded. "He wants to come home, I know he does." She looked at me, her face puzzled. "Why won't they let him?"

Uneasily I stared at her, not sure what to say or think. As the silence in the kitchen grew, Daphne came clickety-clacking down the hall. Without a word, she scooped Hope into her lap and hugged her tight. "It's all right," she said tenderly. "You know how confused Grandmother gets, Hope. Daddy's not coming back, no matter what she says. He's dead, Hope. You know that."

Hope nodded, but she didn't look up from Daphne's shoulder. "He would if he could, though, wouldn't he?" she mumbled.

Daphne nodded. "But he can't, Hope, he can't. And we have to take care of ourselves." She sat there, with Hope on her lap, and finished drinking her tea. Then she got up. "Come on, Hope. Get your jacket. We'll walk partway down the drive with Jessica."

Nine

AFTER LEAVING Daphne and Hope at the foot of their driveway, I hurried home. I wanted to get as far away as possible from Mrs. Woodleigh and her talk about dead men coming back.

By the time I reached Willow Court, I was breathless from running and half-frozen. As I pushed our front door open, I heard Josh's stereo blasting away upstairs, but for once the noise didn't irritate me. Compared to Daphne's house, full of the sound of wind and creaking shutters, Josh's stereo was positively comforting.

While I was fixing myself a peanut butter and jelly sandwich, I heard Josh thumping downstairs. "Where have you been all day, Jess-o?" he asked. "Mom's called twice, and she was upset because I didn't know where you were."

"I went to see Daphne," I said.

"I thought you didn't like her. Isn't she the one you said was so weird?"

"That was before I got to know her." I frowned at Josh. "She's actually very nice."

"What's in the envelope?"

"The illustrations for our book." After washing my hands, I opened the envelope and spread the pictures out on the table. "Aren't they beautiful?"

Josh stared at the paintings. "Did she really draw these?"

I nodded, proud of Daphne. "She's a wonderful artist, isn't she?"

"She sure is." He examined each one, and then he grinned at me. "If your story is just half as good as these pictures, you'll win for sure."

Mom walked in before I'd put the pictures away. "These are beautiful, Jessie." She studied them, smiling and shaking her head. "Daphne has real talent."

"I know." Returning the illustrations to the envelope, I said, "Mr. O'Brien was right when he said she wouldn't let me down."

"What are we having for dinner?" Josh opened the refrigerator and scowled. "There's nothing to eat!"

Mom smiled. "I'm going to the store tomorrow, Josh. Ed's taking us out to dinner tonight."

Josh groaned. "Where's he taking us? If it's not McDonald's, I'm not going."

"We were thinking about the Magic Skillet. You've never had crepes."

"And I don't want any. All I want is a Quarter-Pounder." Josh scowled. "What are crepes anyway?"

"They're fancy pancakes with stuffing." I was happy to know something Josh didn't know for once. "They're really good."

85

"They sound horrible," Josh grumbled. "Do I have to change my clothes?"

Mom and I looked at his T-shirt, a souvenir of a Purple Punks concert he'd gone to last summer, his faded jeans, and his frayed running shoes.

Mom nodded. "Go up and put something decent on. That nice tan sweater and your brown cords. Ed will be here in a few minutes. She looked at me. "You, too, Jessica. How about your striped sweater and the slacks I bought to go with it?"

When Ed arrived, both Josh and I passed inspection. Although Josh was still grumbling about burgers and fries, Ed and Mom loaded us into the back seat of Ed's Datsun and whisked us off to the Magic Skillet.

Of all the restaurants I've ever been to, the Magic Skillet is my favorite. It overlooks a big, man-made lake where you can rent paddleboats in the summer, and it has a nice, cozy atmosphere. The waitresses dress like Heidi, and if you order a Coke they put a cherry in it. I was determined not to let Josh ruin the evening by complaining about the food.

While Josh quizzed Mom about the menu, I tried to remember what I'd had the last time. Tracy's parents had taken us out to dinner for her birthday, and I'd ordered something with chicken in it. But what? Three crepes listed chicken as an ingredient. As I deliberated, I could hear Josh muttering that everything was too fancy. He finally decided on a ham and cheese crepe, and I ordered Chicken Divan, hoping I'd like it.

While we waited for our food, Mom told Ed about Daphne's pictures. Turning to me, she asked if I'd found out why Daphne had missed school last week.

"She has mononucleosis," I said.

"Oh, that's awful. How long will she have to stay home?"

"She doesn't know."

"Well, I hope someone gets a tutor for her." Pausing to take a sip of water, Mom asked me about Mrs. Woodleigh. "Did you meet her?"

I nodded, glad to see our waitress arriving with our food. I felt uncomfortable at the prospect of talking about Mrs. Woodleigh. I had a feeling Mom wouldn't want me to visit Daphne if she knew how strange her grandmother was.

Thanks to Josh, the conversation never got back to Mrs. Woodleigh. He monopolized the evening talking about a new video game he'd played at the arcade. "See, the whole object is to keep these green invaders out of the fortress, but they're really tricky."

Josh went on and on, describing every method he'd discovered to blast the little green things. Ed's eyes practically glazed over with boredom, but Josh didn't stop talking until he'd eaten his way through a salad, a bowl of soup, two crepes, and a strawberry blintz heaped high with whipped cream.

When I gave Mr. O'Brien Daphne's pictures on Monday, he was delighted. "These are beautiful," he said. "I certainly wish Daphne were here, though. When is she coming back to school?"

"She has mononucleosis," I said, "and she doesn't know when she'll be back."

"But what is she going to do about all the work she's missing?"

"I told her I could bring her assignments," I said.

"Well, that's very good of you, Jessica, but she should have a tutor." Mr. O'Brien stroked his beard thoughtfully. "Maybe I could drive out there one day after school and talk to her grandmother. She may not know that the Board of Education will supply free tutoring for Daphne."

He looked at his calendar and shook his head. "Looks like I'm all booked up this week. Will you see Daphne any time soon?"

"I told her I'd go out there on Saturday."

"That's great. I'll send a letter along with you, telling Mrs. Woodleigh how to get a tutor."

On Saturday, I slipped the mice into my pocket, grabbed Mr. O'Brien's letter and Daphne's assignments, and walked out to Cook's Lane. Luckily for me, the weather had warmed all week, and it felt more like spring than winter.

Daphne and Hope were waiting for me by the mailbox, and we walked up the driveway together.

"Did you bring the mice?" Hope asked.

With a flourish, I pulled them out of my pocket and held them toward her in the palm of my hand. Happily she snatched Baby Mouse and capered about laughing and squeaking.

"Let's go to the grove," Daphne said.

"Giving the house a wide berth, we entered the grove and began working out the details of our sequel.

"This is the Forest Savage," Daphne intoned, "and it is here that we must search for Sir Benjamin. The perils are many, my lady, and you must have courage." She walked Cragstar up the trunk of the fallen tree, and I made Princess Heatherfern follow.

After an hour or so, Hope came scrambling up to join Daphne and me in our perch high in the tree. "Let's ask Grandmother for something to eat," she said. "Me and Baby Mouse are hungry."

Daphne's face clouded over and she shook her head. "She hasn't gone to the store yet. I don't think we have anything for lunch."

"I've got my allowance with me," I said. "Let's go to McDonald's. We can walk to the one on Route 210."

Hope's face lit up. "Oh, let's, let's!" She bounced so hard the branches swung up and down wildly.

"I don't have any money," Daphne said.

"That's okay. I've got enough for all of us," I said.

It took me at least ten minutes to persuade Daphne to let me treat, but she finally gave in.

"We should have brought the cart, Daphne." Hope poked in the weeds along Cook's Lane, dislodging bottles and cans with her toe. "Look at all this stuff."

Daphne seemed embarrassed. "We can come back with Grandmother sometime."

"What does she do with all those newspapers and bottles and things?" I asked.

"There's a junkyard down the road. They pay her for it." Daphne walked a little faster.

"Yes, we make lots of money that way," Hope said.

"Not lots, Hope," Daphne said sharply.

"Enough to buy our groceries," Hope insisted.

As we rounded a curve, I saw the intersection, and

89

a little farther down the road McDonald's golden arches. "There it is," I said.

Inside I had to argue with Daphne about what to order. She kept insisting that all she wanted was an order of french fries and a glass of water, but I knew she was hungry. She was picking the cheapest thing because she didn't have any money. I finally persuaded her to have a hamburger and fries, but I couldn't talk her into anything else.

Hope, on the other hand, ordered a Big Mac with cheese, a large order of french fries, and a strawberry milkshake.

Just as we were finishing our food, I looked out the window and saw Tony and Scott pedaling into the parking lot on their ten-speeds. Quickly I got up and mumbled something about going to the ladies' room. I was hoping that if I stayed in there long enough, the boys would be gone when I came out.

Congratulating myself on my quick wits, I ducked inside without being seen and went into a stall. A few seconds later, I heard someone else come in. Looking down, I saw two pairs of running shoes.

"Oh, no, somebody's in there," I heard Michelle say.

"Look at my hair!" The second voice was Tracy's.

Inside the stall, I cringed. What were they doing here? I'd only seen Tony and Scott. From them I would have been safe in the ladies' room, but now I was really trapped.

"I look awful," Michelle groaned.

"Me, too," Tracy said. "If Tony and Scott didn't ride

so fast, it wouldn't be so bad. I thought we'd never catch up with them."

"Did you see Daffy when you came in?" Michelle started laughing.

"No, is she here?" Tracy sounded surprised. "I thought she was sick or something."

"She was sitting at the table near the door with a funny-looking little kid." Michelle snorted. "She didn't look sick either. Not physically, at least. Mentally, that's another story."

Then the door opened again. Little feet this time in dirty sneakers with a hole in one toe.

"Jessica, aren't you ever coming out?" Hope squatted down and peered under the door at me. "Are you sick or something?"

Flushing the toilet, I opened the door. Michelle and Tracy, who had been busily writing their names on the mirror with lipstick, stared at me, their mouths open in amazement.

"Jessica!" Tracy said. "What are you doing here?"

I shrugged. My face was so red, I thought my skin was going to burst.

Then Tracy looked at Hope. "Are you Daphne's little sister?"

Brushing some of her hair out of her face, Hope smiled sweetly at Tracy and Michelle. "Uh-huh. Do you go to school with her and Jessica?"

Tracy nodded and shot Michelle a look over Hope's head. Michelle was laughing as usual. "What's wrong with your sister? How come she hasn't been in school?" Tracy asked innocently.

"Grandmother doesn't want her to go. She says Daphne's so smart she doesn't need to go to school."

"Is that right?" Michelle flipped her hair back and examined her face in the mirror.

"How about you, though? Don't you go to school either?" Tracy asked.

Hope shook her head. "I'm just in kindergarten, so I don't need to. Grandmother says all you learn there is finger painting and silly songs. I already know how to read, so it would be a waste of time."

"Gee, you and Daffy sure are lucky to be so smart you don't have to do the things everybody else has to do." Michelle's voice was loaded with sarcasm.

Hope looked up at me. "Come on, Jessica, let's go."

"Are you with Daphne?" Tracy asked.

"I had to bring her her homework," I said stiffly.

Hope gave my hand a tug, and Michelle snorted. "You better go on, Jessica. You don't want to keep Daffy waiting."

As soon as we left the ladies' room, Hope asked, "Did that girl call Daphne 'Daffy'?"

"I didn't notice." Anxious to leave, I hurried past Tony and Scott without looking at them. "Where's Daphne?" I asked Hope.

"I don't know." Hope followed me out into the parking lot. "She was sitting at our table when I went to get you, and those boys started talking to her. Don't they like Daphne?" Hope looked very worried. "You like her, don't you?"

"Of course I do, Hope." I led her across the lot and up the road. Far ahead of us, I could see Daphne striding along.

"Daphne, Daphne!" Hope shouted and started running up the road after her. "Wait for me!"

At the sound of Hope's voice, Daphne turned around, her arms folded tightly across her chest. When we caught up with her, I could tell that she had been crying.

"What's wrong, Daphne?" Hope caught her sister's hand and stared up at her.

Daphne shook her head. "Nothing." Without looking at me, she started walking away, yanking Hope after her. "Come on, Grandmother is probably worried to death about us."

Ten

ALTHOUGH DAPHNE was making it very clear that she had no wish to speak to me, I tagged along behind her and Hope, trying to think of something I could say to make everything all right.

When we reached the driveway, Daphne turned around and looked at me. "Thanks for bringing me my homework and treating us to lunch." Her voice was stiff and formal, and she didn't smile.

I shrugged. "That's okay. It wasn't any trouble." I wanted to apologize for hiding in the ladies' room, I wanted to beg her not to hate me for deserting her, but I just stood there, fiddling with my glasses and feeling miserable.

"Well, Hope and I have to go home." Daphne hesitated.

"Okay." I put my glasses back on and shoved them into place on my nose. "Do you want me to bring your homework next Saturday?"

"I don't care. If you want to." Daphne gazed past

me at the clouds blowing across the sky, but Hope kept staring at me as if she were trying to figure out what was going on.

"Can't Jessica come have tea with us again?" Hope looked up at Daphne.

"I think Jessica probably wants to go home," Daphne said in a low voice, still not looking at me.

Daphne started walking up the driveway toward her house. I waited for her to look back, to say something. When she didn't, I called, "Are you mad at me?"

She glanced over her shoulder. "What makes you think I'm mad at you?" Her voice was cold and unfriendly.

"Because of what I did." I looked down at the ground, ashamed to face her. "I'm sorry I went to the ladies' room," I mumbled. "It was a dumb thing to do."

When Daphne didn't answer, I raised my eyes. She was standing in the same place, her back to me.

"I said I'm sorry!" I yelled, beginning to feel annoyed. I was apologizing, wasn't I? What more did she want?

Daphne spun around then. "You just didn't want them to see you with me, did you?" Her face was full of hurt and anger, and her voice trembled.

I shook my head, but I couldn't deny it. "You don't understand, Daphne." Even to me, my voice sounded whiny.

"Oh yes, I do." She glared at me. "I hate Adelphia and I hate that school and I hate all the kids who go there. I'm never going back, never!" Her eyes filled with tears, and she tried to wipe them away with the back of her hand.

"When you get well, you're coming back, aren't you?"

She shook her head vigorously. "I'm not sick, there's nothing wrong with me at all. I lied to you about having mononucleosis." Losing the battle against her tears, Daphne buried her face in her hands and sobbed.

Hope put her arms around Daphne's waist and hugged her. "Don't cry, Daphne, don't cry. Grandmother said you didn't ever have to go back to that school. Remember? She said it was a bad school."

"But Daphne," I said, "it's against the law not to go to school. You can't just stop going."

Daphne sighed. "You don't understand, Jessica. It's not just Tony and Scott and Michelle. It's more than that."

"What is it? What's wrong?"

Daphne shrugged and gazed past me at the sky. "There's no sense in telling you because there's nothing you can do. There's nothing anybody can do." She looked as if she were about to cry again, and Hope patted her arm protectively.

"It can't be that bad, Daphne," I said apprehensively.

"If I tell you what's really wrong, will you promise not to tell anybody? Not your mother, or Mr. O'Brien, or anyone?" Daphne looked at me solemnly.

I nodded. "You can trust me," I whispered, hoping she really could.

"Well," Daphne hesitated as if it were hard for her to go on. "It's my grandmother. I'm really worried about her. She's getting stranger and stranger, Jessica. I'm afraid to leave her alone."

"Why?" Daphne's pale face frightened me. "What do you think she'd do?" My mind was racing with images of madness, things I'd read about in books, scenes I'd watched on television late at night.

"You heard the things she was saying about Daddy and the house falling down. She scares Hope to death talking like that. Little kids don't know what to believe. They get so confused."

"But couldn't Hope go to kindergarten?"

"That's only half a day, Jessica." Daphne shook her head. "I can't leave Hope alone with her."

I tried to think of something to tell Daphne, some good advice, a solution to all her problems, but my mind refused to produce a single idea. "Couldn't we talk to my mother? She'd know what to do."

"No. You promised, Jessica, you promised not to tell anyone!" Daphne stared at me, her eyes begging me not to betray her.

"But you can't just stay home. Someone will find out, and you'll get in trouble. You could get taken to court or something."

"Not if everyone thinks I'm sick. Don't you understand, Jessica? If you tell your mother, Hope and I will end up in an orphanage, and they'll put Grandmother in a mental hospital." Daphne began to cry again, big sobs that shook her whole body.

"I won't tell anyone, Daphne, I promise." I patted her arm clumsily, and Hope hugged her, but she didn't stop crying for a long time.

Finally she wiped her eyes on her sleeve and blew her nose. "I'm sorry, Jessica. I didn't mean to be such a crybaby, but I'm so scared and worried." She gave me a shaky, lopsided grin and scooped Hope up into her arms. "It's okay, Hopesy. I won't cry anymore."

Hope planted a big, wet, noisy kiss on Daphne's cheek and tweaked her nose. "You be happy, Daphne, or I'll punch you."

Daphne laughed and twirled round and round with Hope on her hip. Their hair swung out, and when Daphne put Hope down, they both staggered a little, dizzy from the spinning.

"I wish I could think of some way to help," I said.

"Just bring me my homework and keep everybody convinced that I'm really sick. Don't let anybody find out about Grandmother." She looked at me earnestly. "Please?"

Still wishing I could persuade her to let Mom help, I promised Daphne I wouldn't tell anybody. "You don't hate me, too, do you?" I asked her, remembering what she'd said about Oakcrest and the kids who went there.

Daphne shook her head. "You're not like the rest of them. I thought you were at first, but I know now that you're different. You're smart, for one thing. And you write wonderful stories."

We smiled at each other, and Hope skipped around us, singing one of her Baby Mouse songs. Above our heads tall clouds, white on the top and purple on the bottom, swept across the sky, trailing their shadows over the field.

Looking down the driveway toward the house, I was startled to see Mrs. Woodleigh hobbling toward us. She was walking in and out of cloud shadows, her hair blowing in white tufts around her face like milkweed silk bursting out of its pods.

"Daphne and Hope," Mrs. Woodleigh cried when she saw us. "Where have you been?"

Before Daphne or Hope could answer, she grabbed each one by an arm and gave them a little shake. She was trembling and her voice was shrill with fright. "Don't ever go away like that again! I've been so worried. You know all the awful things that happen to young girls!"

As Daphne started to apologize, Mrs. Woodleigh noticed me. For a second she stared at me, bewildered, as if she'd never seen me before. In the sunlight, her face looked terribly old and fragile, deeply etched with wrinkles and quivering with anger.

"It's you again, is it?" She stepped closer and waved a clenched fist at me. "You go home, girl, and don't come back here again. I know your kind, leading my children away, teaching them your Adelphia ways. You're a bad girl, a bad girl! Go on, now, get off my property!"

I backed fearfully away, and Hope thrust herself between her grandmother and me. "No, no, don't make Jessica leave!"

Mrs. Woodleigh grasped Hope's shoulders. "Don't you tell me what to do!"

"Let me go, let me go! You're hurting me," Hope cried.

As Hope struggled to escape, Mrs. Woodleigh fell down on her knees and hugged Hope to her bosom. "No, baby, don't. Don't turn against me."

Daphne touched Mrs. Woodleigh on the shoulder. "Come on, Grandmother. Let's go home," she said softly.

Releasing Hope, who was now in tears, Mrs. Woodleigh got up stiffly, her face full of misery. Without looking at me, she allowed Daphne to lead her away.

Not knowing what to do, I watched the three of them walk down the driveway. When they reached a curve, Daphne looked back and waved, and Hope called, "Come back soon, Jessica!"

As I walked slowly home, I asked myself again and again what I could do to help Daphne. Confused and unhappy, I paused on the footbridge near our house. If there were only someone I could talk to, someone who would know exactly what to do.

Below the bridge, the creek gurgled over stones, swirling and frothing, carrying little twigs and bits of trash along with it. Glancing at the place on the bank where Daphne and I had built a little shelter for the mice, I saw that someone or something had wrecked it. The twig roof was scattered and the stone walls were broken. Reaching deeply into my pocket, I caressed the three mice. I was glad they hadn't been in the shelter when it was destroyed.

The sun set slowly behind our townhouses and the air lost its warmth as I trudged slowly up the hill toward home. When I opened the front door, I heard Mom and Ed laughing in the kitchen. They were working on dinner together, chopping up peppers and onions and making silly jokes like a couple of teenagers. Luckily they were more interested in each other than they were in me. It wouldn't have taken much attention from Mom to make me break down and tell her everything. I wanted to talk to her so badly, but I had to keep my promise. I'd let Daphne down too many times already.

* * *

Sunday dragged by in a gray mist of rain, and I kept myself busy working on a book report for English and studying for a science test. By the time I went to bed, I had convinced myself that I was getting sick and would not have to go to school on Monday.

Unfortunately it was a lot harder to convince Mom that I was sick. Like it or not, I had to go to school, and that meant I had to face Michelle and Tracy.

To postpone seeing them as long as possible, I dawdled over my breakfast and then walked to school as slowly as possible. When I got to the playground, I knew I was late. There wasn't a person in sight, and all the buses were gone. For a minute I was very upset because I knew I'd have to go to the office for a pass, but then I realized that I'd saved myself from meeting anyone in the hall. Nobody would be waiting by my locker to tease me about McDonald's.

By avoiding making eye contact with anyone, I got through the first two periods without any problems, but my luck ran out in English. Mr. O'Brien had gone over our stories and drawings and decided that most of us were ready to bind our books.

Since Daphne, of course, wasn't in school, I had to do ours all by myself. All around me, I could hear the other kids laughing and talking as they worked. Never had I felt so lonely.

It was almost a relief when I saw Michelle and Tracy walking toward me. For a few minutes they stood without speaking, one on either side of me, watching me bind the book. Michelle was so close to me that I could smell the bubble gum she was chewing.

I tried to pretend I didn't see them, but Michelle finally popped her gum so loudly that I jumped.

"Been to McDonald's lately?" Michelle's voice had an icy edge.

I shook my head and tried to concentrate on my book.

"What were you doing in there? Spying on us?"

I stared at Michelle, genuinely surprised. "Why would I spy on you?"

She shrugged. "Maybe you wanted to find out what Tracy and me were doing with Tony and Scott." She stared back at me from under purple eyelids.

I shook my head. "I wasn't spying, honestly."

"But you were with Daffy, weren't you?" Michelle persisted.

I pressed my book carefully into its cover. Without looking at her, I nodded.

"Are you getting to be friends with her?" Tracy asked.

"She's not so bad, you know," I mumbled. "Really, when you get to know her, she's pretty nice." But I didn't look at either one of them.

"Daffy?" Michelle snorted.

I could feel my face getting redder and redder, and I shoved my glasses back onto the bridge of my nose.

Michelle leaned closer to me. "She's not really sick, is she? I mean not physically. She looked perfectly healthy to me."

"I think she's just hooking school," Tracy added. "Her little sister said she was too smart to go. That sounds like hooking to me."

"She has mononucleosis," I said, "and it takes a long time to get over it. Hope was just confused."

At this, Michelle burst out laughing. "Daffy has mono? Are you kidding?"

"What's so funny about that?" I stared at Michelle, puzzled.

"You know how you get it, don't you?" Michelle continued to laugh.

When I didn't say anything, Michelle shook her head and rolled her eyes at Tracy. "You get it from kissing," she said. "It's called the kissing disease. Who would kiss Daffy?"

"That's not true. You get it from drinking out of the same glass, not from kissing!" I glared at Michelle.

But she and Tracy just laughed. "Maybe she kissed Donald Duck!" Michelle almost swallowed her gum cackling at her own joke.

As she started quacking and making kissing sounds, Mr. O'Brien walked up to us. "What's going on here?" He frowned at Michelle.

"Nothing." Michelle stopped laughing and gave me a nasty look.

"Have you two finished binding your book?" he asked.

Tracy nodded and held it up for him to see. "Does it look okay?"

Mr. O'Brien took "The Nightmare Slumber Party" and flipped the pages. "Fine, it looks fine." Handing it back to Tracy, he told her and Michelle to go back to their seats.

When they were gone, he looked at "The Mysterious Disappearance of Sir Benjamin Mouse." Patting my arm, he smiled. "It looks beautiful, Jessica, really lovely. Is Daphne feeling any better?"

I nodded, ashamed to look at him. It was one thing to lie to Michelle, but Mr. O'Brien was different.

"Did you talk to her grandmother about the tutor?"

"I gave her the letter," I said uneasily.

"I hope she gets one soon. I'd hate to see a girl as intelligent as Daphne fail a grade." He smiled at me. "Next time you see Daphne, tell her I miss her and I'm looking forward to having her return to school. Maybe I'll drop by her house one afternoon and see how she's doing."

I nodded, and he moved on to another desk to check the work Tony and Scott were doing on their war story. As I put the finishing touches on my book, I hoped Mr. O'Brien wouldn't have time to drive out to Daphne's house. One look at Mrs. Woodleigh would probably send him to the Board of Education, and then Daphne and Hope would end up in an orphanage for sure.

Eleven

WEDNESDAY EVENING I was in my room doing my math homework when the phone rang. Josh bellowed up the stairs that it was for me, so I put down my pencil and went to answer it.

To my surprise, it was Daphne. "I thought you didn't have a telephone," I said.

"I'm at the pay phone at McDonald's." Daphne's voice sounded high and worried.

"You didn't walk there, did you? Not by yourself?" I was horrified. It was dark and cold outside.

"It's not far." She paused, and I could hear a car start up and drive away. In the background, cars roared past on Route 210.

"Aren't you freezing?" I pictured the pay phone outside McDonald's with nothing around it to shelter it from the wind.

"A little." Daphne paused again, her voice uncertain. "I just wanted to talk to somebody. Hope and Grandmother are both asleep, and I got kind of lonely."

I twisted the telephone cord around my finger and tried to think of something interesting to tell her. Here she'd walked all the way to McDonald's in the dark and the cold just to talk to me, and I didn't know what to say. "We bound the books Monday," I finally blurted out, "and ours is definitely the best one in the whole class. Mr. O'Brien loves it, and he told me to tell you he misses you."

"Did he really say that?" Daphne sounded pleased.

"Yes. He sent all the books off to be judged yesterday, and he said we'll probably hear early in April."

"That's a long time from now," Daphne said. "What are you doing in English?"

"We're finishing up grammar and we're starting a unit on poetry next week. That should be a lot more interesting."

"Yes," Daphne said. "I like poetry."

"Me, too."

There was another silence. "Would you be able to come out and see me after school tomorrow?" Daphne finally asked. "I know it's a long walk, but maybe your mother could pick you up after she gets off work."

She sounded so lonely that I couldn't refuse. "Will you meet me at the mailbox?" I asked.

"Are you sure you don't mind? I don't want you to come if it's inconvenient or anything." Daphne's voice was filled with uncertainty.

"No, no, it's fine. I'd like to come," I said. "I'll bring the mice."

"Thanks, Jessica. I'll see you tomorrow." Daphne sounded happier.

After I hung up, I went to my room and looked out

the window. It was almost ten o'clock, and the night looked cold and scary. I tried to imagine Daphne walking along Route 210, cars speeding past her, their headlights flashing across her face. Picturing Cook's Lane in the dark, I shivered. The very thought of being alone in the night frightened me, and I hoped that Daphne would get home safely.

When I left school on Thursday, the weather had turned raw and cold. The sky was heavy with dark clouds, and the wind had a damp, cutting edge that pierced my parka and chilled my bones. By the time I got to Cook's Lane, I was cold all the way through.

As I reached the top of a hill, I saw Daphne and Hope waiting for me, huddled together by the mailbox. Their parkas were the only color in the wintry landscape of brown fields and gray skies.

"Did you bring them?" Hope ran to meet me and seized my hands. "Is Baby Mouse in your pocket?"

I pulled him out and gave him to her, and she capered away, squeaking her Baby Mouse song. Daphne and I looked at each other and laughed at Hope.

"You're so silly, Hopesy-Dopesy!" Daphne ran after her sister, and tried to tickle her, but Hope squirmed away, giggling, and darted ahead of us toward the house.

"Do you want to come inside for a while?" Daphne asked. "Grandmother's asleep now. She doesn't usually wake up until four or four-thirty. I'll fix you a cup of tea."

"Are you sure she won't wake up?" While I hesitated, a gust of cold wind buffeted me. The icy edge of it took my breath away, and I decided to risk encountering Mrs. Woodleigh.

Very quietly we slipped into the house. While Daphne fixed tea, I played with one of the cats, and Hope crawled around the floor with Baby Mouse. I knew they both wanted me to enjoy myself, but it was hard to relax, knowing that Mrs. Woodleigh was upstairs. Every creak the house made sounded like her getting out of bed and coming downstairs.

"I like those ribbons in your hair." Hope leaned against me and toyed with the ribbons hanging from my barette. "They look pretty."

"Thank you, Hope." I gave her a little hug. She felt tiny, all bones, but she snuggled against me happily and walked Baby Mouse up and down my arm.

Daphne put our teacups on the table and sat down. "Did you bring me any homework?"

I pulled some sheets of paper out of my pocket and smoothed them flat. "This is our poetry assignment."

She looked at it and smiled. "That looks like fun."

"It is." I handed her another sheet. "This is math homework."

She frowned. "I hate math."

"Me, too."

Hope stirred sugar into her tea and smiled at me. "Can we go to your house after we finish our tea?" she asked me.

Daphne looked shocked. "Hope, you don't ask people things like that. And besides, you know we can't leave Grandmother here by herself."

Hope frowned. "Grandmother is a grownup, isn't

she? We don't have to take care of her all the time." She twirled a long strand of hair around her finger. "Besides, I'm hungry. Maybe Jessica's mother would invite us to stay for dinner."

"We have our own dinner right here, Hope!" Daphne sounded very upset.

"Just cereal. I'm tired of cereal, Daphne. And we don't even have any milk. She fed it all to the cats." Hope got up and opened the refrigerator door. "See? There's nothing to eat."

"There's soup and tuna fish and Dinty Moore stew." Daphne's face was flushed.

"No, there's not." Hope climbed up on the counter and opened the cupboard. "One box of corn flakes, that's all. And some pickles."

"You don't have any food?" I stared at Daphne, horrified. Josh and I loved to complain to Mom that there was nothing to eat, but it was never really true. We meant there weren't any doughnuts or cookies or strawberry yogurt. But here I could see for myself there was nothing on the shelves or in the refrigerator.

"She must have fed it all to the cats." Daphne looked as if she were going to cry.

"My mother would be glad to give you dinner," I said. "When she comes to pick me up, you can just come home with us. Mom wouldn't mind a bit."

But Daphne shook her head. "We can't leave Grandmother. It upsets her too much."

"But what will you eat?"

"The cereal." Daphne shrugged. "I guess we should be glad that cats don't like cereal."

"I want a real dinner, like our mommy used to fix. I don't want cereal!" Hope started to cry. "And I don't want to live here anymore!"

Daphne scooped Hope up into her lap and tried to comfort her. "I'm sorry, Hope, but we have to stay here. We can't leave poor Grandmother all alone. Please try to understand."

"Do you have money to buy food?" I stared at Daphne, trying to understand.

"Grandmother gets Social Security checks, but she hasn't felt well enough to go to the bank to cash them. Right now all we have is what we get for the bottles and cans. I haven't got much more than a dollar."

"And soon we aren't going to have any gas or electricity," Hope said, "because she won't pay the bill. But Daddy's coming back soon, and then everything will be all right."

I looked at Daphne. "What's she talking about?"

Before Daphne could say a word, Hope continued, "Grandmother saw him in the woods yesterday, and he told her that he was coming home soon."

"Hope, I told you not to believe Grandmother. You know Daddy can't come back." Daphne shook Hope gently. "Grandmother imagined she saw Daddy. She didn't really see him."

"Grandmother wouldn't lie!" Hope's face was white, her eyes enormous. "Daddy is coming back, he has to! What will happen to us if he doesn't?"

Daphne shook her head. She was crying now. "Hope, Hope, please, everything will be all right. I can take care of us, I can do it. I won't let anything happen to you."

Just then Hope froze. "Grandmother's awake, she's getting out of bed."

All three of us looked at the ceiling. Sure enough, I could hear footsteps, slow and faltering, on the floor overhead. Jumping up from the table, I pulled on my parka. "Listen, I better leave before she comes down here. Do you all want to come with me?"

"We can't." Daphne hugged Hope, trying to keep her from running after me.

"Please come." As I fumbled with my zipper, I could hear someone walking downstairs. I didn't want to run away like a coward, but I was afraid to face Mrs. Woodleigh.

"No, we can't, Jessica." Daphne's eyes pleaded with me to understand.

"Well, good-bye, then." I hesitated, my hand on the door knob.

"Who's this?" Mrs. Woodleigh appeared in the doorway, clutching a soiled bathrobe around her thin body. "I thought I told you not to come here, girl!" She glowered at me fiercely.

"It's Jessica, our friend." Hope looked worriedly at her grandmother. "She wants us to have dinner at her house, but Daphne says we can't." Hope's lower lip trembled and her eyes filled with tears.

Mrs. Woodleigh took a tottering step toward me. "I know what you want, you can't fool me. Your father's one of those fast-talking Adelphia real estate men, isn't he? He sent you out here to soften me up so he can get my property. Well, it won't work. I won't sell. Not for any price." She shook her fist at me, inches from my nose. "Now, go on home. Get out of here!"

111

"Jessica's our friend!" Hope shouted. "She doesn't want our farm. She doesn't even have a father!"

"Doesn't have a father?" Mrs. Woodleigh looked at me, her face filled with sympathy. "Why do the fathers always go away? Is he over there in Vietnam too?"

"He's in California," I whispered.

"California?" Mrs. Woodleigh sounded confused. "Are they keeping them in California now?"

"He just lives there," I said. "He and my mother are divorced."

The old woman frowned. "I might have known. That's all Adelphia is. Divorce, alcohol, drugs, sex, crazy stuff." Sniffing loudly, she sat down at the table. "Well, where's my tea?"

Daphne grabbed a cup. "I was just going to fix it."

As she turned to the stove to check the kettle, I whispered, "I better leave now, Daphne."

"Oh no, not yet. You haven't finished your tea." Hope tugged on my arm. "And we haven't played mice. Please stay just a little longer, Jessica."

"Tea looks awful strong!" Mrs. Woodleigh scowled at the cup Daphne had set before her. "I bet it doesn't even have sugar in it." She took a sip and made a face. "When will you ever learn to do it right?" Dumping two or three heaping spoonfuls into her cup, she began drinking noisily.

"I'm going to walk partway down the driveway with Jessica," Daphne said.

"That's right. Leave me here all alone to drink my tea. What does it matter? I'll be dead and gone soon enough." Mrs. Woodleigh stared into her cup. "See my tea leaves? You don't have to be a gypsy to read them. Here's one little one all by itself. That's me. All the others are going somewhere together, leaving me all alone."

Hope bent over the cup. With one dirty little finger, she pushed the lonely tea leaf over with the rest. "Now you're with all the others, Grandmother. See?" Hope smiled at Mrs. Woodleigh.

"Humph." The old woman didn't return the smile. "Where are you going?" Her sharp tone stopped Hope as she started to follow Daphne and me out the door.

"With them," Hope said, her smile fading.

Mrs. Woodleigh's hand shot out like a claw and grabbed Hope's arm. "No, no, baby. You stay here with Grandmother. It's too cold out there for you." She drew Hope close to her. "You love your grandmother, don't you? You don't want to leave me all alone in the shadows with that crack running over my head."

Hope looked uncomfortable. "Can't I come?" she asked Daphne.

"Stay here, Hope. I'll be right back."

"You aren't going to play mice?"

"Not today," I said.

"Then here." Hope held Baby Mouse out to me. "Take him."

"You can keep him for a while, Hope. I'll get him next time." With relief, I heard Daphne open the door. I slipped out behind her, glad to escape from Mrs. Woodleigh.

"Are you sure you can't come home with me?" I asked Daphne as we walked down the driveway.

113

"I told you no!" She looked angry and unhappy.

"But what are you going to do? You've got to have food and electricity and heat!"

"I'll get the checks cashed. I can forge her name if I have to. And we have plenty of wood for a fire and candles for light. We can get along just fine!"

"But she's crazy!" I screamed at Daphne. The word came out without my even thinking. "She's crazy and you know it! How can you live with a crazy person?"

"Don't ever say that again!" Daphne's voice was tight and tense. "She's just old, she's not crazy." With tears running down her cheeks, Daphne glared at me. "Just go on home. I don't need you or anybody else!" Turning her back on me, she ran up the driveway toward the house.

I started to run after her, but Mrs. Woodleigh opened the door and peered out into the dusk. Seeing me, she shouted, "Go on now, girl, get out of here!"

This time I did what she told me to. As I ran down the driveway, stumbling on the rutted ground, I could see the lights of Adelphia twinkling through the dusk like stars. I ran toward them, anxious to reach the safety and comfort of my own house.

Twelve

WHILE MOM and I were cleaning up the kitchen after dinner, I decided to risk asking her a few things. Clearing my throat, I said, "Do all people get kind of crazy when they get old?"

She looked a little surprised by my question. I guess she couldn't imagine what had prompted it. "No, of course not, Jessie. Think of your grandmother. She goes to Europe every summer, she does volunteer work at the hospital three days a week, she has lots of friends. Why, she actually has a more active social life than I do."

"Yes, but she's not really old." I thought of my grandmother, her hair nicely set, well dressed, always ready to share a joke or a good story. And then I thought of Mrs. Woodleigh in her shabby bathrobe, her hair wild, talking about dead men coming back and houses falling down on her head.

"Your grandmother is seventy-three years old, Jessie. She's not exactly a teenager." Mom took the last cup out of the dishwasher and set it on a shelf.

"Well, she doesn't look that old. Or act it."

"That's because she takes good care of herself. She exercises, she watches her diet, she keeps herself busy."

"But some people get crazy when they're old, don't they?"

"It's called senility, Jess-o." Josh opened the refrigerator door, surveyed its contents and shook his head. "Nothing to eat," he groaned.

"How do you get it?" I stared at Josh, the boy genius and walking encyclopedia.

"It's caused by hardening of the arteries. Arteriosclerosis." He dragged the word out, glorying in its many syllables, showing off his awe-inspiring vocabulary. "Your arteries get all clogged up with animal fat and your brain can't get enough blood, so your brain cells start dying. Zap, zap, zap."

Mom frowned. "You make it sound like a video game."

"I didn't invent it." Josh bit into a huge peanut butter and jelly sandwich, dribbling strawberry jam down the front of his shirt.

Trying not to look at the jam on his chin, I asked him if there was a cure for senility.

He shook his head, his mouth stuffed with bread. Swallowing noisily, he said, "Brain cells can't be regenerated. Once they die, that's it. So you just get worse and worse."

"That's awful," I said.

"Maybe you better cut down on the cholesterol," Mom said, watching him pour a glass of milk.

Josh shrugged. "The world will have ended in a nuclear war long before my arteries get a chance to clog up."

On that happy note, Josh left us. In a few seconds, I could hear his video game beeping, bipping, and zapping. Picking up Snuff, I told Mom I was going upstairs to study.

Friday night Josh called me to the telephone. It was almost ten-thirty, and the four of us were watching an old Alfred Hitchcock movie on television. Grabbing a handful of Ed's special hot buttered popcorn, I left the room reluctantly, hoping I wouldn't miss too much of the movie.

It was Daphne.

"Are you at McDonald's?" I pulled the phone as far away from the living room as the cord would stretch.

"Yes. I had to wait till Hope fell asleep before I could sneak out." She paused, and I could hear cars and voices in the background. "I wanted to apologize for shouting at you yesterday." Her voice sounded small and faraway. "I was upset."

"That's all right. I shouldn't have said what I did, either."

"Are you coming over tomorrow? I'll understand if you don't want to."

"Of course I'm coming." I glanced at Mom and Ed, but they were too interested in the movie to eavesdrop on my conversation. "Did they turn off the gas and electricity yet?"

"This morning. But it's not too bad. We have a big fireplace in the living room, so we moved our beds down there. It's cozy with the firelight and the candles."

"How about food? Did you cash her checks?"

"Not yet, but Hope and I collected a lot of bottles, enough to buy hot dogs and bread and milk. You don't have to worry about us, Jessica." Her voice was getting an edge to it, and I was afraid she was going to get mad again.

"Besides," she went on, "winter is hard on old people. Grandmother will be better in the spring."

I thought about what Josh had said about arteries and brain cells, but I didn't say anything to Daphne about it. Instead I said I'd see her at two o'clock on Saturday.

"I'll meet you at the mailbox," she said. "We'll go for a walk. I found a wonderful place, Jessica. It's a long way, but it's worth it."

She paused again while a car drove past. "I have to go now. If Hope wakes up and finds I'm gone, she'll be terrified."

"Be careful walking home, Daphne. It's so late."

"Don't worry. I can take care of myself."

After she hung up, I stood there in my warm, safe kitchen. Josh, Mom, and Ed were laughing at a commercial on television, Snuff was rubbing round my ankles, hoping for a handout, and the cuckoo clock over the sink was striking eleven. I was glad that I wasn't walking along a dark road all by myself, and I hoped that Daphne really could take care of herself.

"Who called you so late?" Mom asked as I snuggled up next to her on the couch.

"Oh, it was just Tracy." I bent my head over Snuff, petting her to avoid looking at Mom. I hated lying to her, but I couldn't imagine what she would think of Daphne's being out alone this late at night. Snuff rewarded my attention by growling and struggling to escape. "How did the movie end?"

"Oh, it was great, really great," Josh said. He launched into a detailed description of everything I'd missed, making Mom forget all about the telephone call.

On Saturday, I walked out to Daphne's, glad that the sun was shining and the wind wasn't blowing. As she'd promised, she was waiting by the mailbox, alone this time.

"Where's Hope?" I asked.

"I didn't tell her you were coming. She thinks I'm out looking for bottles, and she's keeping Grandmother company. Come on." Daphne ran off across the field, and I followed her into the woods.

Taking a winding path, she led me through trees and around boulders, climbing uphill steadily. It was lovely in the woods. High up in the bare branches the wind blew gently, and underfoot the ground was soft and rustly with leaves. Squirrels scampered about, and bluejays and crows exchanged cries overhead.

At last we reached the top of the hill and stepped out of the woods. We were standing on the edge of a cliff. Down below us, the Patapsco River wound its way through a narrow valley, glittering in the winter sunlight.

"Isn't it beautiful?" Daphne swept her arm across the sky.

I nodded. "I feel like Daniel Boone exploring the wilderness."

119

Daphne smiled and sat down on a shelf of rock. Dropping down beside her, I rested quietly, letting the sun warm my back.

"Look, Jessica!" Daphne pointed at a bird circling above us, wings spread. "It's a red hawk."

I watched the hawk drifting up and down on gusts of wind, high above the river and the valley.

"It must be wonderful to be a bird, to be able to fly like that." Daphne sighed. "If people really get reincarnated, I'd like to come back as a bird. A hawk or a sea gull. Something wild and free."

"I think I'd never come down to earth," I said. "I'd sail on the wind forever."

We sat in silence then, watching the hawk until it veered away from us and finally vanished, a tiny speck in the sky.

After a while I remembered the sandwiches I'd made before I'd left home. "Are you hungry?" With a flourish, I presented the sandwiches and a couple of apples.

"You didn't have to bring food." Daphne looked embarrassed instead of pleased.

"I know, but walking makes me hungry." I bit into a peanut butter and banana sandwich that Josh himself wouldn't have found too small. Gesturing at the other one, I said, "Go on, Daphne, eat it."

She shrugged and picked it up. "I am pretty hungry," she admitted. "Grandmother gave the rest of the hot dogs to the cats."

"You better get those checks cashed."

Daphne nodded. "If the weather stays like this, Grandmother might get to the bank next week. In the

120

cold, her rheumatism bothers her, and she can hardly walk."

I shook my head sadly, thinking of my own grand-mother. If only Mrs. Woodleigh were like her. Life seemed so unfair sometimes.

As we were finishing our apples, I asked Daphne where she'd lived before she came to her grandmother's house. It was something I'd been wondering about. She'd never really said anything about her mother or her earlier life, and I was curious.

Without looking at me, Daphne gazed off into space. "In Boston," she said.

"With your mother?"

She nodded.

"Did you like it there?"

She nodded again. Looking more closely at her, I realized that she was crying.

"I'm sorry, Daphne. Did I say something wrong?" Ashamed of myself, I huddled on the rock beside her, wishing I hadn't given in to my curiosity. I should have realized that Daphne would have mentioned her past before now if she had really wanted to talk about it.

Daphne shrugged and tried to wipe her eyes. "My mother was driving home from work. It was raining. There was this truck—the driver didn't see her car." Daphne took a deep breath. "She never came home."

My stomach felt quivery just thinking about it. Suppose something like that happened to my mother? I couldn't imagine what it would be like never to see her again. To say good-bye to her in the morning, never dreaming it was the last time. A sharp lump rose in my throat and tears stung my eyes. Silently I stared at

Daphne, but she sat, her face turned away from me, looking at something I couldn't see.

"Then they sent us to Grandmother in July. I guess they thought she was the best person to take care of us." Daphne's voice was flat and lifeless.

"You didn't have any other relatives?"

Daphne shook her head. "Neither my mother nor my father had any brothers or sisters, and my mother's parents died before I was born. She did have some cousins and aunts, I think, but I never met them. They lived in Maine. That's where she was born."

"Maybe there's some way you could find them."

Daphne looked at me. The wind played with her hair so that strands of it lifted and fell around her face, making it hard to read her expression. "What's the use?" she asked dully, turning away from me to gaze across the valley.

"Well, I was thinking that if anything happened to your grandmother, if she got worse or something, maybe you could live with them. Then you wouldn't have to worry about foster homes and things like that."

Daphne sighed. "I told you Grandmother will be better in the spring." Daphne tossed her apple core far out into the air and watched it fall down into the valley. "Maybe an apple tree will grow down there, and I'll come back and find it when I'm grown up."

"What are you going to be when you grow up?" I asked, wanting to change the subject to something more pleasant.

"An illustrator, of course." Daphne smiled at me. "And you're going to be a writer. We'll do all our books together, and we'll live in Boston. I know just the street.

We can share an apartment in an old townhouse, the kind with a walled-in garden behind it. My studio will have a skylight in the ceiling, and we'll hang plants everywhere."

I stretched out flat on the rock and smiled up at the blue sky. "My den will have a skylight, too, and we'll have lots of cats. A black one, a marmalade one, a calico, a tabby, and a couple of Siamese."

"We'll give parties, and the people who come to them will all be artists and writers."

"We won't know anybody like Sherry and Michelle and Tony."

"No. Our friends will be smart and interesting." Daphne laughed. "Like us. Right?"

I laughed too. "Right."

"And we'll never get married and live boring lives. We'll just have men friends. Lots of them. And they'll all smoke pipes and talk about philosophy and be desperately in love with us."

It was such a daring thought that I laughed even harder. "You're crazy, do you know that?"

"Sure. Crazy people are lots more interesting than normal people. Just look at Sherry and Michelle." She wrinkled her nose and sprang to her feet. "Come on, Jessica, we'd better start walking back."

Taking a long, lingering look at the valley below us, I turned and scrambled over the rock behind Daphne. A crow flew by overhead, cawing, and somewhere below us a dog barked.

About halfway down the hill, we stopped to rest on a fallen tree. Suddenly Daphne laid a hand on my arm and pointed. About fifteen feet away, a deer stepped out of the trees. She paused and sniffed the air. Neither of us made a sound as she moved gracefully down the bank of a small stream and bent to drink the water. Behind her, two more deer appeared, another doe and a young stag. They, too, drank from the stream. Then, sniffing once more, the three of them waded across the stream and vanished among the trees.

"I've never seen a real deer before," I whispered.

"I saw one once standing in the woods, so still I thought I was imagining him. But he wasn't nearly as close as they were." Daphne turned to me, her eyes shining. "Maybe it's an omen. Maybe it means something good will happen to us."

I nodded. "Let's always be very quiet when we're in the woods. Maybe we'll see them again."

Like Indians, we slipped off the limb and walked as silently as we could, trying not to rustle the fallen leaves. As we reached the edge of the woods, I looked across the field toward the road. "Is that Hope down there by the mailbox?"

Daphne nodded. "I told her not to leave Grandmother alone!" Breaking into a run, she dashed across the field toward Hope.

"Daphne!" Hope cried. "You didn't tell me Jessica was coming!"

"Why aren't you home with Grandmother?" Daphne sounded angry.

Hope frowned. "She fell asleep, and I got lonesome. I came out to look for you. You said you were getting more bottles and cans." Hope looked accusingly at Daphne.

"I did. Look." Daphne climbed down into a gully

124

and pulled a black plastic garbage bag out of the bushes. From the clunking sounds inside, I could tell it was full of bottles.

"Will it be enough to buy more hot dogs?" Hope asked.

"I think so. A small pack at least. Or a jar of peanut butter."

"I'd rather have hot dogs." Hope smiled at me. "Want to go to McDonald's, Jessica?"

I shook my head. "I don't have any money, Hope." Reaching into my pocket, I pulled out my last sandwich. "Do you want this?"

Hope took it and bit right into it. "Thank you," she said, her mouth full of peanut butter.

"Was Grandmother feeling all right?" Daphne asked Hope.

Hope nodded. "She's happy because Daddy's coming home soon, maybe tomorrow, she said."

"Don't talk like that, Hope," Daphne said sharply.

"It's true." Hope smiled. "She saw him this morning on the front porch."

"She didn't see anyone, Hope." Daphne frowned. "You can't see someone who's dead."

"He's not dead, Daphne. They never sent his body back. He was missing, not dead. And now he's coming home." Hope wiped her mouth with the back of her hand and licked her fingers. "Next time, can mine have jelly on it, Jessica?"

Daphne bit her lip. "Hope, you have to understand. In Vietnam lots of soldiers died, but no one found their bodies, so they were called 'missing.' They were really dead, though. Daddy is dead. He can't come back."

"Then how come I saw him, too, Miss Smarty?" Hope put her hands on her hips and stared up at Daphne, her eyes gleaming. "He was standing there, I saw him. So there!"

"Oh, Hope." Daphne knelt down and put her arms around Hope. "Daddy would come home if he could, and so would Mommy. But they can't, Hope, they can't!"

Angrily Hope pulled away. "I saw him! I saw him!" she screamed. "Grandmother told me where to look, and I saw him!" Turning around, she ran down the drive toward the house, her hair swirling around her shoulders.

"Daphne, what's she talking about?" The air around me seemed full of ghosts and my scalp felt prickly.

Daphne shook her head. "It's Grandmother. She's talked about seeing Daddy so much that Hope's getting as crazy as she is." She clapped her hand over her mouth. "I didn't mean that! She's not crazy, she's just, just . . ."

Daphne's voice trailed off and she looked away from me, toward the house, at Hope running up the steps and opening the door. "I love my grandmother," she whispered. "I really do."

"I know." I patted her arm.

"She will get better in the spring, Jessica. Won't she?" Daphne looked at me, her eyes wide and wet with tears.

"I hope so." Dropping my eyes, I stared at the ground. I couldn't tell her what Josh had said. She was too upset already.

"I better go see if Hope is all right. I don't want her

to upset Grandmother." Daphne backed away, down the drive, lugging the plastic bag. "Thanks for coming to see me. I'm glad we saw the deer and the hawk."

"Me, too." I watched Daphne back farther away, wanting to do something for her, but not knowing what.

"Will you come back next Saturday?" she asked.

I nodded. "Maybe I'll come out one day after school, too, if the weather stays warm."

"Okay." Daphne smiled and waved. "'Bye, Jessica."

"'Bye." For a few seconds I stood still and watched her hurrying toward the house, bumping the plastic bag along behind her. Then I turned away and walked slowly home.

Thirteen

As THE MONTH of February dragged itself by, I walked out to Daphne's house at least once a week, sometimes after school and always on Saturday. Once in a while we took Hope to McDonald's, but usually we climbed the path through the woods to our favorite spot above the Patapsco Valley. We saw the hawk almost every time, but we never saw the deer again, no matter how quietly we walked.

Although I always took the mice with me, we didn't play with them unless Hope was along. We usually had too many things to talk about. Sometimes Daphne shared her worries about her grandmother with me, but more often we discussed books we'd read or daydreamed about our future as a great author-illustrator team.

One of our favorite pastimes was making fun of Michelle and Sherry. Daphne could imitate them perfectly. She made me laugh until my sides ached, prancing around and saying exactly the sort of dumb things they said.

On my long walks home from her house, I often wondered how I'd gotten along without Daphne to talk to. Never had I known anyone who made me feel so comfortable. Around her, I didn't have to worry about being immature or odd. As she said, our talents made us different from other people, but not strange.

"And besides," she liked to say whenever I was feeling depressed about something Michelle had said or done to me, "all artists and writers have unhappy childhoods. They have to suffer. It's what makes them creative."

The only cloud on the horizon of our friendship was Mrs. Woodleigh. The weather was getting better, but she wasn't. If anything, she was getting worse. And Daphne wouldn't face it. No matter how irrational her grandmother was, Daphne insisted that she was just having a bad day. I couldn't say a word against Mrs. Woodleigh without upsetting Daphne, so I had to bite my lip and keep my thoughts to myself.

One afternoon late in February, Daphne invited me into the house. It was a cold, blustery day, the sort that drives people inside. After convincing me that her grandmother was asleep, Daphne led me quietly upstairs.

Most of the rooms were empty. The wind rattled the windows in their frames, and strips of wallpaper, coming loose from the wall, fluttered in the drafts. The house was hardly any warmer than the front yard, and we roamed from room to room, searching for a cozy corner.

Pausing by an old trunk in a room lined with stacks of newspapers, Daphne opened the lid.

"Want to see what my grandmother looked like a long time ago?" She lifted a pile of photographs from a box and motioned me to sit down beside her.

I studied the brownish pictures spread out on the floor. A pretty girl, looking very much like Daphne, smiled up at me. Sometimes alone and sometimes in a group of laughing people, Mrs. Woodleigh posed happily for the camera.

"She was so pretty," I whispered. It seemed tragic that Mrs. Woodleigh had once been young and happy, that she had never dreamed that one day she would be an old woman in a cold, dark house, full of misery and fear.

Daphne nodded, her face sad. I knew she was thinking the same thing I was thinking.

Shuffling through the photographs, she pointed to a picture of a handsome young man. "This is my grandfather. And look, here's Grandmother holding my father when he was a baby."

On and on the pictures went, telling the story of Mrs. Woodleigh's life. Gradually the baby grew, and the man and the woman got older.

"This is my mother," Daphne whispered, showing me a group of wedding pictures.

"She looks just like Hope, doesn't she?" I handed the photos back to Daphne, and she laid them aside. Everyone seemed so happy clustered around the smiling bride and groom that I couldn't bear to look at them.

"And—ta-da!—here I am!" Daphne showed me a fat little baby held aloft in her father's arms.

There were a few more pictures of Daphne, growing from a laughing baby into a solemn little girl with long hair. The last photograph was of her father, wearing an army uniform.

"Well, that's it." Daphne scooped up the pile of pictures and dumped them back into the box. "My family history."

As Daphne put the box in the trunk, we heard footsteps pattering down the hall toward us. I clutched Daphne's arm, terrified of encountering Mrs. Woodleigh.

But it was only Hope. "Look, Jessica." Kneeling next to me, she showed me what she was carrying. "Callie had kittens yesterday. Did Daphne tell you?"

"Oh, can I hold him?" I held out my hands, and very carefully, Hope laid a tiny black kitten in them.

"His eyes aren't even open," she whispered, stroking his head lightly with one small finger.

"He's beautiful," I sighed. "How many did she have?"

"Five, but he's the only black one. All the rest are tabbies."

I laid my cheek next to his back, loving the soft, fluffy feel of him. "I've always wanted a black cat." As I patted him gently, I heard him purr, a tiny rumbling sound almost too loud to come from such a little creature. "If you were mine, I'd name you Raven," I told him, "because you're black all over and very beautiful."

"Do you want to keep him?" Hope asked.

"I'd love to, but we have Snuff. I don't think Mom would let me have two cats."

"Snuff needs a friend," Hope said. "Raven could keep her company."

"But how about your grandmother? Maybe she wouldn't want me to take him."

"Considering how many cats we already have, I doubt she'd miss him," Daphne said.

"Besides, it will be one less cat to eat our hot dogs," Hope said.

That evening I asked Mom about the kitten.

"Oh, Jess, we have one cat. Isn't Snuff enough?"

I frowned at Snuff quietly washing herself in a corner of the room. "You know what a grump she is. This kitten is so sweet and pretty. I just know he'd grow up to be the kind of cat who sits on your lap and purrs. And I'd do everything. Feed him and change his litter box and clean up any mess he makes. You wouldn't have to do anything, Mom. Please?"

Mom smiled. "Well, I'll think about it. Snuff is getting old and crotchety. It might be nice to have a kitten around the house."

I hugged her. "You're the most wonderful mother in the whole world!"

"Especially when I say yes, right?" Mom hugged me back. "But don't blame me if Snuff eats him for dinner!"

The first day of March came roaring in like a lion on a rampage, bringing snow and sleet and all sorts of horrible weather. I couldn't go to Daphne's for a whole week. She called me a couple of times from McDonald's, though, to keep me up to date on the kitten's progress.

"It's getting warm, isn't it?" Hope asked the next

time I saw them. "Soon it will be spring and Daddy will be here for sure. It's just the bad weather that's making him stay away."

Ignoring Hope's remark, Daphne looked at me. "Jessica and I are going to take a long walk, Hope."

"Can I come, too?" Hope capered about. "We could play mice. We haven't done that for a long time." She took Baby Mouse out of her pocket. "Where's Princess Heatherfern?" She walked Baby Mouse up my sleeve.

"I didn't bring her." I smiled apologetically at Hope.

"You go on home and keep Grandmother company," Daphne said to Hope.

"No." Hope shook her head vigorously and frowned. "She scares me when she talks about the crack. And she's asleep anyway. I want to go with you and Jessica."

Daphne sighed. "We're climbing up to the rocks, Hope. The last time you came with us, you fussed and complained about being tired."

"I won't get tired this time, I promise!" Hope ran ahead of us across the field. "Come on, come on! You can't catch me, I'm the gingerbread man!" she shouted.

Daphne and I ran after her and caught her easily. "Now remember, be quiet in the woods and we might see the deer," Daphne cautioned Hope as she led us silently up the path.

Although we didn't say a word until we reached the top of the hill, we didn't see a sign of the deer. I was beginning to think they'd left the woods or that something awful had happened to them, but I didn't mention my fears. At the very thought of hunters, I knew Hope would begin to cry.

Pulling apples and sandwiches out of my pockets, I passed them around. For a long time, we sat quietly, eating and watching the clouds sail by.

"It feels like spring today, doesn't it?" Daphne asked. "The trees in the valley look so soft. I wish I could reach out and stroke them. They'd feel like big cats."

"The clouds, too," Hope said. "See that one? It's a little fluffy lamb that's lost its mommy and it's all alone." Hope looked at the sky sadly, her attention focused on one cloud drifting along all by itself near the horizon. "It's like me," she added.

"No, it's not." Daphne put an arm around Hope and hugged her. "You have me."

"I miss Mommy." Hope looked up at Daphne. "If Daddy comes back, will he bring Mommy with him?"

Daphne shook her head. "No, Hope."

Hope pulled away and sat down on a rock by herself. "Poor little cloud," she said to the sky.

Daphne stood up. "We'd better go back. Grandmother shouldn't be alone too long."

"I want to stay here," Hope said.

"Then you'll have to stay all by yourself," Daphne said. Without looking at Hope, she started down the path.

Worriedly, I took Hope's hand. "Come on. You don't want to sit here all alone."

Yanking her hand away, Hope frowned at me. "Yes, I do. I want to be all by myself. Nobody loves me anyway."

"Daphne loves you, Hope." I looked over my shoulder, but Daphne was already out of sight. "Come on."

She shook her head. "No."

"Jessica," Daphne called from somewhere in the woods. "Are you coming?"

"Hope," I implored.

"Just leave her there," Daphne called again.

Uncertainly, I tried counting, a technique I'd seen mothers use at swimming pools, in department stores, at tot lots, wherever children loitered. "One, two, three." My voice rose pleadingly. "When I get to ten, I'm leaving."

"I don't care." Hope turned her back.

"Four, five . . ." I counted. At ten nothing happened. "Well, good-bye, Hope, I'm going."

She didn't respond, but Daphne called again. Slowly I walked across the rocks to the path, glancing back frequently at Hope. She just sat there, her back still turned to me.

When I caught up with Daphne, I smiled apologetically. "Do you think it's all right to leave her there all alone?"

"What do you think she's going to do? Throw herself off a rock?" Daphne sounded cross. "She's doing it to get attention. She likes you to feel sorry for her. It makes me mad when she acts like that."

I sighed, still worried about Hope, and followed Daphne down the path. I noticed she was walking a lot slower than usual. Every now and then she would pause and look back. At the sound of a branch snapping, she smiled.

"Don't look now, but she's following us. I knew she wouldn't stay there by herself," Daphne whispered.

By the time we reached the edge of the woods,

Hope had gotten over her sulks. "Don't go home yet, Jessica," she said. "Come with us and see the kitten. He's almost big enough to go home with you."

"Not quite," Daphne said. "He should stay with his mother for another three weeks. Why don't you wait here, Jessica? I'll go get him."

"Can I stay with her?" Hope took my hand and smiled up at me.

"Of course." Daphne ran off across the field, and Hope launched into a long Baby Mouse story, complete with sound effects and a funny little dance.

Just as Hope was beginning her account of Baby Mouse's escape from Big Ike, the meanest cat in the whole world, she stopped jumping about and pointed toward the house. "Look, here comes Daphne."

We watched Daphne running toward us, her hair flying. She looked worried, and before she was halfway across the field, she started shouting. "She's not there, Hope, she's not there!"

"Callie ran away? Did she take the kittens?" Hope cried.

"Not Callie—Grandmother!" Daphne stopped, gasping for breath. "I went in to see if she was awake, and she wasn't in bed. I looked all over the house, but she wasn't anywhere."

"Where would she go?" I asked.

"To look for Daddy," Hope said.

"Of course!" Daphne said. "Where does she go when she takes you out to look for him?"

"I'll show you." Hope ran back toward the house, and we followed her. Taking a path through the woods

136

behind the barn, we came to an old road, just two ruts, really, leading away across a field.

"Are you sure this is the right way?" Daphne stopped and scanned the landscape for a sign of her grandmother.

Hope nodded. "Sometimes we walk real far, and then Grandmother gets lost and I have to show her how to get home."

Daphne sighed and squeezed Hope's hand. Avoiding the puddles left from last week's bad weather, we walked silently, hoping to see Mrs. Woodleigh around each bend in the road.

It was obvious that we had entered some sort of unofficial junkyard. All around us were rusting castoffs. Gap-doored refrigerators, wrecked cars stripped to their frames, and gutted television sets lay scattered in the weeds as if they'd fallen from the sky.

Uneasily I glanced over my shoulder, half-expecting to see someone following us, but I saw no one. Just the empty road, its puddles shining in the sunlight.

"We should have brought bags with us," Hope said. "Look at all these cans and bottles."

"We can come back sometime," Daphne said. "After we find Grandmother."

"There she is, I see her!" Hope pointed ahead. "She's talking to Daddy."

Mrs. Woodleigh was sitting on an overturned washing machine, her back to us. Her whole body was tense, and she was gesturing excitedly. "You must come now, John!" she was saying. "I don't care what they say, we need you, we need you!" Stretching out her hands to someone or something only she could see, she didn't notice Daphne and Hope hurrying toward her.

I hung back, afraid to go near Mrs. Woodleigh. She looked wilder, crazier than usual. Her hair blew in the breeze, and her voice swept loudly across the field, as harsh and rasping as a crow's. Over her bathrobe she wore her old red plaid lumber jacket, and on her feet were a pair of large, untied workboots. Between the frayed hem of her nightgown and the top of the boots, I could see her bare legs. They were thin and pale and splotched with veins.

"Grandmother!" Hope threw her arms around the old woman. "Why didn't you wait for me?"

Startled, Mrs. Woodleigh pushed Hope away and heaved herself to her feet with great effort. "See what you've done!" she cried, her voice shrill with grief. "You've frightened him away!"

Turning toward the empty field, Mrs. Woodleigh shrieked, "John, John, come back, come back!" She spun about, this way and that way, her face filled with despair. "Don't leave me, please don't go away again!"

Weeping, she struck at Hope, lost her balance, and fell to her knees. As Daphne rushed to help her up, Mrs. Woodleigh grabbed her and shook her. "You wicked girl, see what you've done? He was about to take my hand and come home, but you scared him away." Clinging to Daphne, she began to cry. "Why won't he stay, why won't he? Wasn't I a good mother to him? I tried, I did my best, why does he hate me? I need him, I need my son."

Daphne helped her to her feet. "It's all right, Grandmother, it's all right. I'm here. I can take care of you."

"No, no. What can you do? You're just a child. We need John." Mrs. Woodleigh shook her head, weeping. "If only he'd come back to us."

"Let's go home, Grandmother. It's going to be dark soon." Daphne gently pulled Mrs. Woodleigh toward the house.

"No, you go. Take the baby and go home. I'll wait here for John. He'll come back, I know he will." Mrs. Woodleigh tried to sit down on the washing machine.

"Please, Grandmother, please. We have to go home." Daphne's voice quavered.

"Grandmother, I'll give you till I count to ten, and then I'm going to leave you here," Hope said. "One, two, three," she counted as slowly as I had up on the rocks.

"Come on, we'll have tea and build up the fire, and I'll read you the next chapter of *Great Expectations*." Daphne took her grandmother's hand. "It's getting cold, and the moon's out already." She pointed to a small crescent hanging low in the late afternoon sky.

"Four, five, six," counted Hope.

Mrs. Woodleigh looked from one to the other, shaking her head, her face confused. "I get so upset sometimes," she said softly. "I can't understand why they won't let him come home. I know he wants to." Slowly she walked along next to Daphne, allowing her to lead her as if she were the child and Daphne the adult.

Keeping well behind, I followed them back to the house. Mrs. Woodleigh hadn't noticed me, and I didn't want her to see me now. By the time Daphne led Mrs.

Woodleigh up the back steps, the sun had set and the sky was washed with pale pink at the horizon. The warmth of the day was gone, and I shivered.

Through the kitchen window, I saw Daphne, a candle in her hand, talking to her grandmother. A few seconds later, the back door opened and Daphne slipped out.

"I just wanted to say good-bye," she whispered. "I'm sorry it's so late. I know you don't like to walk home after dark."

"It's all right." I stared at her pale face. "Is she going to be okay now?"

"I think so."

"I wish you could come home with me. Have dinner and stay overnight. You and Hope both."

Daphne sighed. "I wish I could, too, but you know I can't."

The door opened and Mrs. Woodleigh stepped out on the porch. "Is that you, John?" she called.

"It's just me, Grandmother." Daphne ran up the porch steps and took her grandmother's arm. "Let's go back inside now, okay? The water will be hot enough for your tea soon."

Then the door shut and I was alone in the dark. Fearfully I ran away from the house, down the driveway, toward Cook's Lane and home.

Before I'd gotten halfway to Adelphia, a car picked me up in the glare of its headlights and pulled off the road. "Jessica!" Ed shouted.

Weak-kneed with relief, I got into his car. "I was at Daphne's and it got dark all of a sudden. I'm sorry."

"Your mother was worried to death." Ed frowned at me.

"I'm sorry," I said again and burst into tears.

"Now, now." He patted my shoulder. "Don't cry. It's all right."

Starting the car, he turned toward home. I was glad to let Daphne's house slip away behind us in the dark. I wanted to forget about Mrs. Woodleigh and John. I didn't want to think about Daphne and Hope sitting around the table, shivering in the candlelight. I just wanted to go home and have dinner and maybe play a game of Clue with Mom and Ed and Josh.

Fourteen

WE ONLY HAD a half-day of school on Wednesday. I had planned to walk out to Daphne's house, but the weather had turned cold and nasty again, the way it often does in March. As I headed slowly away from the school, trying to decide whether I wanted to walk all the way out to Cook's Lane in the cold, I saw Tracy waving at me.

Since she was by herself, I caught up with her. She had acted a lot friendlier in the last couple of weeks, and I thought she had gotten over being mad at me.

"Where have you been lately?" Tracy asked me.

"Just around," I said nonchalantly.

She looked at me closely. "Are you still taking Daphne her homework?"

I nodded.

"You know, I heard Mr. O'Brien and Miss Kaufmann talking about her yesterday. I think they're going to send somebody out there to see what's going on."

"What do you mean?"

Tracy shrugged. "Well, her grandmother never got a tutor for her, I heard Mr. O'Brien say, and she's missed a month of school."

"Daphne can't help being sick, and she's smart. She's done all the homework I've brought her."

"But what about her tests? She's missed a lot of tests." Tracy stopped and put her hand on my arm. "She's not really sick anyway, is she? I haven't forgotten what her little sister said in the ladies' room about Daphne being so smart she didn't need to go to school."

I frowned. "You don't understand, Tracy. There's a lot you don't know about Daphne. If you did, you'd feel sorry for her."

"What do you know?" Tracy stared at me as if she were really interested.

"Just things." I stared back at her, remembering my promise not to tell.

"Hey, Tracy!" Michelle and Sherry hurried up the path toward us. "We're going to the village center. Want to come?"

"Sure." Tracy looked at me. "Why don't you come with us, Jess?"

Not wanting to walk away all by myself, I nodded. I still felt awfully uncomfortable around Michelle and Sherry, but I was glad that Tracy had invited me.

"Seen Daffy lately?" Sherry asked me.

"Her name is Daphne," I said coldly.

"Oh, pardon me!" Sherry rolled her eyes at Michelle, and they both started laughing.

"Look," Tracy said, pointing at a couple walking across the softball field. "There's Keith with Shannon. Didn't I tell you he broke up with Lissie?"

"What a jerk!" Sherry narrowed her eyes and scowled at Keith.

"What does he see in her? Lissie's much prettier. And a whole lot nicer." Michelle frowned.

"Shannon's a dog if you ask me," Sherry said. "And she's fat."

For several minutes, they ripped Keith and Shannon to shreds, and I walked along feeling safe for the time being. I caught Tracy's eye once and smiled at her, thanking her silently for coming to my rescue.

When we got to the village center, we went to the gift shop and browsed around, looking at jewelry and reading funny greeting cards. A saleslady kept following us, asking if we needed help. From the way she looked at us, I think she must have thought we were shoplifters. She seemed disappointed when we left without stealing anything.

"Come on, let's go look at makeup in the Food Barn," Michelle said. "I need some new lip gloss." She led us into the grocery store.

While Michelle and Sherry went off to find the lip gloss, Tracy and I walked over to the candy section. I was trying to choose between a Snickers bar and a pack of Reese's Pieces when I heard a familiar voice in the next aisle.

"But I love olives," Mrs. Woodleigh was saying, her voice rising in a quavering wail. "Don't put them back. Please let me have them, just this one time."

"We can't afford them, Grandmother. We need peanut butter, and we don't have enough money for both," I heard Daphne say.

"I hate peanut butter." Mrs. Woodleigh was whining like a child. "I don't want to spend my money on something I hate. I want the olives!"

Tracy looked at me. "Did you hear that?" She sounded a little scared.

I nodded and picked up the Snickers bar, no longer really caring what kind of candy I bought. "Come on, let's go," I said to Tracy. "I promised my mother I'd do the laundry and start dinner before she came home." I started walking toward the express line, hoping we could get out of the store before Tracy saw Daphne and her grandmother.

"Wait a minute, Jess. I haven't decided what I want yet." Tracy sounded annoyed.

"I've got to go home, Tracy." Getting more and more nervous, I edged toward the checkout line.

"I won't let you put the olives back!" Mrs. Woodleigh shouted, still out of sight. "John may be here for dinner, and he loves olives!" Her voice rose above a loud Muzak arrangement of "All You Need Is Love."

Picking up her candy bar, Tracy walked toward me. "Maybe we should get out of here. That person sounds crazy."

Just as we caught up with Michelle and Sherry at the lipstick display, we heard a terrible crash and the sound of breaking glass.

"Now see what you made me do!" Mrs. Woodleigh screamed.

The store manager left his little office and headed for Aisle 4, along with just about everyone else in the whole store. Michelle said, "What's going on?" and followed the crowd.

"Come on, Tracy!" Grabbing her arm, Sherry towed

145

Tracy along behind her. "Let's go see the olive lady."

Reluctantly I followed them, but when we got to Aisle 4 I ducked behind a display rack filled with pantyhose. Hoping I wouldn't be seen, I peeped cautiously around the edge of the rack. There was Mrs. Woodleigh, ranting and raving about the olives, her big work boots planted firmly in a sea of debris.

"She made me do it, it was all her fault!" Mrs. Woodleigh pointed at Daphne, who was frantically trying to gather up the olives and broken glass littering the floor.

Hope clung to the grocery cart, her eyes wide with fright. "It wasn't Daphne's fault, it wasn't!" she cried shrilly, but no one paid any attention to her.

"It's all right, ma'am, it's all right. There's nothing to worry about," the manager said to Mrs. Woodleigh. "Just calm down. Why, anybody can have an accident. It happens all the time." He bared his teeth in a tight little smile and patted Mrs. Woodleigh's arm.

A man carrying a mop and bucket pushed his way through the crowd of shoppers gathered around the Woodleighs. As Daphne moved out of his way, she looked straight at me. Sure that she was about to speak to me, I shook my head and stepped back behind the pantyhose display.

Although I was ashamed of myself, I hid like a coward among the L'eggs Eggs, my face burning. I wanted to help Daphne, but I couldn't force myself to walk past the people watching Mrs. Woodleigh's performance. I knew they would all look at me, waiting to see what new entertainment I was going to provide. I hated myself, but I didn't take a step toward Daphne. Not one.

Instead I slammed the candy bar down on a shelf and ran out of the Food Barn, hoping that Daphne wouldn't hate me forever.

I was halfway home when Tracy, Michelle, and Sherry caught up with me. "Where did you go, Jess?" Tracy asked. "We were looking all over the store for you."

"Did you see Daffy's grandmother?" Sherry snorted with laughter. "She's a lunatic!"

"She really had that manager going, didn't she?" Michelle laughed. "There were olives everywhere. It was like an ocean full of little green islands."

"Did you see him give her the jar?" Sherry asked. "I think it was a bribe to get her out of the store."

"No wonder Daffy's so weird. Their whole family must be crazy or something." Michelle looked at me. "Oh, pardon me, I forgot. *Daphne*, I meant to say. I certainly wouldn't want to offend Jessica." Her voice dripped with sarcasm.

"No," Sherry said. "She might sic a mouse on you."

"Why don't you shut up, Sherry?" I shouted. "And you, too, Michelle! You don't understand anything, do you?" Tears started running down my cheeks, and I wanted to slap them both, hard. "How would you like to live with somebody like that?"

They stared at me, too surprised to say anything. Tracy was the first to speak. "She's right, you know. It's not funny. There's nothing to laugh at."

But Sherry and Michelle laughed anyway. "Give me my olives!" Michelle wailed in a high falsetto voice.

"I have to feed my ducklings," Sherry cried.

"And my mice," Michelle added.

"Stop it, you all," Tracy said. "Can't you see how upset Jessica is?" She put her arm around my shoulders. "Come on, Jess, it's okay. Don't cry."

I buried my face in my hands and kept on crying. I was so angry at myself for running away and leaving Daphne that I hardly knew what to do. As much as I hated Sherry and Michelle, I hated myself more.

"Come on, Jess, let's go home," Tracy said.

Without saying another word to Sherry and Michelle, we walked away. Never in my life had I been so grateful for Tracy. Without her, I don't know what I would have done.

When we got to the path that led to Tracy's court, she stopped and looked at me. "Are you okay?"

I nodded, moved almost to fresh tears by the sympathy I saw in her face. "They're so mean. How can they be like that?"

Tracy shook her head. "I don't know. Sometimes I have fun with them, but other times they get so awful I can't stand them." She sighed. "Poor Daphne. I feel so sorry for her, Jess. I wish I'd been nicer to her."

"Me, too."

"But you have been. You took her homework out there and all."

"But I should have helped her in the store. She probably thinks I hate her or something." I felt a new wave of shame as I saw the scene in the Food Barn again. Why had I hidden like that?

Tracy smiled a little uncertainly. "She'll probably understand. You were just scared, Jess. I was scared, too. I never saw anybody act like that."

I nodded. "I *was* scared. Mrs. Woodleigh terrifies me." I hopped back and forth from one foot to the other, trying to get warm. "It's freezing out here."

Tracy nodded. "And it's almost spring. It should be warm."

"I guess I'd better go home. I'll never get all that stuff done for my mother." I looked at Tracy. "Do you think Sherry and Michelle are going to be mad at you?"

She shrugged. "I don't care if they are. The way they were acting made me sick." She smiled at me. "Anyway, I've got other friends. You, for instance." With a wave of her hand, she turned and ran up the path toward her court, and I ran the other way.

When I got home, I found Josh in the kitchen, eating a huge peanut butter and jelly sandwich expanded with raisins and bananas.

"Well, Jess-o, how was your day?" he asked.

"Not too good." I wished I could tell Josh about Daphne. He was older than I was. Maybe he could give me some advice. Not the kind an adult gives, all full of rules and regulations and ifs and buts and complications, but something that would help me.

"What's wrong?" He looked at me, really looked at me, as if it had just occurred to him that I was a human being, too, not just a dumb little sister. "Have you been crying?"

My eyes filled with tears. They splashed down on my sweater and clung to the wool like little drops of dew.

"What happened?" Josh took another bite of his

sandwich, but he still looked interested. He might have been a scientist discovering an unknown quality in a specimen he thought he knew everything about.

"Well, you know Daphne and how we've gotten to be friends and all." I gulped a little from all the crying I'd been doing.

Josh nodded.

"And you know how Michelle and Sherry and their friends make fun of her and call her Daffy Duck and stuff."

"Yeah. Typical middle-school garbage."

"Well, there are things about her I've never told anybody. She made me promise not to." I blew my nose. "She lives with her grandmother, and her grandmother's crazy, Josh. And today in the Food Barn she made this terrible scene."

Ashamed to look at Josh, I told him about the olives and how I'd run away instead of helping Daphne. And I told him about Daphne's father and the cats and the gas and electricity and the crack in the ceiling and Daphne's not going to school. By the time I finished, I was exhausted.

Josh kept shaking his head while I was talking and making little inarticulate sounds. "Jess, this is awful. I mean it's really serious. You've got to tell Mom, you've got to."

"But I can't! I promised Daphne I wouldn't!" I started crying again. "I thought you could help me, I thought you would know what to do!"

"I'm telling you what to do," Josh said. "Those two kids can't go on living with that crazy old lady."

"But they'll get put in an orphanage or something. And they'll hate me."

Josh frowned at me. "Who are you thinking about, Jess? Yourself or Daphne? If you want things to go on getting worse and worse for Daphne, just keep it all a secret. But don't blame me if the old lady dies or the kids get sick or the house burns down when a candle falls over."

I stared at him, horrified. "I never thought of that."

Josh shrugged. "Well, start thinking, Jess-o." He finished his glass of milk in one tremendous gulp, then went upstairs. In a few seconds I heard the Purple Punks blasting down through the ceiling.

Feeling more depressed than ever, I picked up Snuff and collapsed on the living room couch. As usual she hissed and growled until she managed to escape from my loving embrace. So I lay there alone, watching the sky turn from gray to black.

When Mom came home, she flipped on the light. "Jessie, what are you doing lying here in the dark?" She stared at me. "Are you all right?"

Shoving my feet out of the way, she sat down on the couch. "Were you asleep?"

"No, I was just thinking."

"Did something happen at school?"

I shook my head. "Not exactly." I took a deep breath. "You know how Daphne's been absent?"

Mom nodded. "Did she come back today?"

"She's not coming back, Mom, and she's not sick either." There, I'd said it. Whatever was going to happen would happen.

151

"What?" Mom stared at me. "Do you mean she's playing hooky?"

"She has to, Mom. She can't leave Hope alone with her grandmother." While Mom sat there looking stunned, I told her what I'd told Josh.

"Oh, Jessica, why didn't you tell me sooner?" Mom put her arm around me. "Those poor girls. I should have known something was wrong."

"Will they really have to go to an orphanage or a foster home?"

"I suppose something like that will happen."

Mom looked so unhappy that I found the courage to ask her the question I'd been rehearsing for hours. "You know what the perfect solution is, don't you? They could come and live with us! We could fix up the recreation room for their bedroom. It would be so easy." I hugged her hard, sure she'd say yes.

Mom looked at me sadly. "Oh, Jess, we couldn't do that, honey."

"Why not?" I pulled away from her. "There's plenty of room here."

"I couldn't take the responsibility of two more children." She hesitated. "And there's Ed to consider," she added softly.

"Ed?" I stared at Mom. "What's he got to do with it?"

"Well, Ed and I are thinking about getting married. I've been meaning to tell you, but I was waiting for just the right moment." Mom reached out to touch me, but I moved out of her reach.

"He has a daughter, you know," Mom added. "She lives with her mother now, but she sees Ed once a

month. When we're married, she'll probably spend
more time with him."

"What do you mean?" I was angry now. "She isn't
going to live here, is she?"

"No, no, Jessica." Mom looked flushed. "She might
be with us on weekends or for a few weeks in the summer. I meant to tell you all this when everything was
definite." She tried to smile at me. "So you see, we can't
take in Daphne and Hope. I wish we could, but we
can't."

"Hi, Mom." Josh bounded down the stairs.
"When's dinner?"

"I don't know. Not for a while. I haven't even
started it yet."

"But I'm starving." Josh rubbed his stomach and
tried to look woebegone with hunger. "Did Jess tell you
about Daphne?"

Mom nodded. "It's such a pity."

"What are you going to do?" Josh asked.

"I was thinking about driving out there to see how
bad it really is," Mom said.

"No, Mom, don't! Please don't do that!" I clutched
her arm.

"Jessica, something has to be done," Mom said
firmly. "I'll drive out there tomorrow morning."

"No, Mom, no. Daphne will never forgive me!"

"What did I tell you, Jess?" Josh said. "Somebody
has to do something!"

I shook my head, confused. "I thought Mom would
let them live here! I'd never have told her if I'd known
she'd say no!"

Mom grabbed my arms and turned me gently toward her. "You can come with me tomorrow, Jessica, but I have to go out there. I can't possibly allow a situation like that to continue."

"No, I can't go with you, I can't!" I pulled away from her and ran upstairs, slamming my door behind me.

Throwing myself down on my bed, I lay there in the dark and thought about Daphne and Hope alone with Mrs. Woodleigh in that cold, spooky house. No lights to chase away the shadows, no heat, the cats milling around underfoot mewing for food, the ghost of John Woodleigh lurking outside, haunting Hope and her grandmother. Shivering with fear for them, I pulled the covers over myself and watched the moon slide out from behind the clouds, silvering their edges with its light.

Fifteen

THE NEXT MORNING, I made another attempt to talk Mom out of visiting Daphne, but she was determined to go. To make things even worse, she had called Ed and persuaded him to drive out there with her.

"You're still welcome to come, Jessica." Mom looked at me hopefully.

"I can't." Turning away, I grabbed my jacket and books. "It's time for me to leave for school."

Slamming the door behind me, I crossed the court and headed for the footpath. Although the wind was still cold, I could feel spring in the sunlight. There was a faint smell of wild onion in the air, and I thought I saw a robin near the footbridge.

The closer I got to school, the slower I walked. Although I would have liked to see Tracy, I didn't want to run into Sherry and Michelle. To make sure I wouldn't, I turned off the path leading to school and wandered along beside the creek. I knew that I was making myself late, but I didn't care.

When I passed a tot lot, I sat down in a swing and rocked slowly back and forth. Poor Daphne. What was she going to do when Mom and Ed showed up at her front door? I tried to imagine the scene. Mom and Ed standing on the porch, Daphne staring at them, Mrs. Woodleigh yelling from somewhere inside, the cats meowing, Hope asking for a trip to McDonald's.

I wondered if the police would come and take Daphne and Hope and Mrs. Woodleigh away. Would Daphne have to go to a detention center for skipping school? Shuddering, I pumped the swing higher into the air. I didn't want to think about what was happening at Daphne's house.

When I was tired of pumping, I dropped my head back and stared at the sky and the treetops dipping up and down. Slowly the swing lost momentum and finally came to a stop. For a while, I sat still, listening to a mockingbird singing somewhere in the woods bordering the tot lot.

All of a sudden I realized that I had forgotten all about school. Conscience-stricken, I looked at my watch. I was half an hour late. Jumping out of the swing, I picked up my books and started running down the path.

When I was about halfway there, I slowed to a walk. I had a terrible pain in my side from running, and I was gasping for breath. At a fork in the path, I hesitated. If I went straight ahead, I'd get to school in five minutes, but if I turned to the right, I'd be home in no time.

Almost without thinking, I turned to the right. I'd

never skipped school before, and I kept expecting to see a policeman patrolling the path looking for truants. The only person I saw, though, was an old lady walking a dog. She smiled at me and said what a lovely day it was. Then she went on her way as if she saw nothing unusual about my not being in school.

When I got home, the house was so quiet it was spooky. No Josh running up and down the stairs, no stereo blasting rock music, no video game bipping and beeping. Just the cuckoo clock ticking and the refrigerator humming to itself.

A little thump in the kitchen startled me, but it was only Snuff jumping down from the counter. She circled my ankles and meowed hopefully when I opened the refrigerator.

"The only time you like me is when I have food in my hand," I grumbled, letting her jump for a piece of cheese.

She snapped it, almost getting my fingers as well as the cheese, and gulped it down. "Me-row?" she asked politely.

Having nothing else to do, I fed her the rest of the slice of cheese bit by bit, hoping she wouldn't throw it up later. Then I went upstairs to my room and lay down on my bed. Although I'd planned to read or maybe even start another Benjamin Mouse story, I fell asleep instead.

I didn't wake up until late in the afternoon. I knew that Josh was home because I could hear his stereo, but I felt too bad to get up and tell him to turn it down. My head hurt, my throat was sore, and my whole body ached.

By the time Mom came home, I was sure I had a fever. When she called me from downstairs, I answered feebly and begged her to bring me a glass of orange juice.

"What's the matter, honey?" Mom paused in the doorway and smiled at me. She had her hands behind her back as if she had a surprise for me.

"Didn't you bring the orange juice?" I whimpered.

"I brought something else." She crossed the room and stood next to me. "Do you feel well enough for a surprise?"

I nodded. "What is it?"

With a little flourish, she handed me something warm and soft, a little bundle of black fur. "For you— from Hope."

"It's Raven!" I cradled the kitten gently. His whole body vibrated with a purr so loud it was hard to believe it came from something so small. Cuddling him close to me, I smiled up at Mom. "Did you keep him at the library all day?"

She sat down next to me and nodded. "He was so good. He stayed in my office and behaved himself beautifully." Laying her hand on my forehead, she looked concerned. "You're burning up, Jessie."

"I feel awful. I didn't even go to school. I stayed home and slept all day."

"Is your throat sore?"

I nodded. "And I ache all over."

"A lot of people at the library have been out sick with some kind of virus. I guess that's what you have." She got up. "I'll get you the juice and an aspirin. Then I'll tell you what happened this morning."

While she was gone, I petted Raven. I wasn't sure I wanted to know what had happened at Daphne's house. Didn't I feel bad enough already? I just wanted to lie in bed and stroke Raven and wait for my body to stop aching. I didn't want to hear depressing things. I didn't want to worry.

When Mom came back, she gave me an aspirin, and I swallowed it down with juice. Then she sat down on my bed and told me what had happened.

"It was a good thing that I went, Jessica. Poor Mrs. Woodleigh was so confused she could barely remember who Hope and Daphne were. Like you said, she ranted and raved about the cracks in the ceiling and assured me that her son would be home any minute to take care of everything. She was very hostile toward Ed and me. At one point she tried to run us off with a broom." Mom shook her head and sighed.

"But it wasn't just her mental condition that worried Ed and me. She's obviously in poor physical health. I suspect she's suffering from malnutrition, and she may have pneumonia from the sound of her cough." Mom looked at me. "You should have told me sooner, Jessica, you really should have."

I lay back on my pillow, still holding Raven, and shook my head. "You know I promised Daphne not to tell."

"Some things are far too serious to keep to yourself. When I think of those poor frightened girls alone in that cold house with that sick old woman, no food, no electricity, no one to turn to for help . . ." Mom's voice trailed off.

"What happened, what did you do?" I asked.

159

"I left Ed there and drove to McDonald's to call the county Social Services Department. They got Mrs. Woodleigh into a hospital, and a social worker took Daphne and Hope to Roseland."

"What's that?" The pretty name sounded like a cover-up for a terrible place with bars on the windows.

"It's a shelter for children who have no suitable home. I know it must sound awful to you, but at least they'll have warm beds and three decent meals a day." Mom patted my shoulder and tried to smile, but her voice was sad.

"Did Daphne say anything about me?"

There was a brief silence. "No, she didn't, Jessica," Mom said slowly. "She was very upset, especially about her grandmother." She paused again. "Hope found the kitten and brought him to me for you. She said she'd take good care of Baby Mouse."

"Oh, Mom." I started crying. "Daphne hates me, doesn't she? She'll never forgive me for telling you, I know she won't!"

"Now, now, Jessie, don't cry. Give Daphne a little time. She'll understand that it was the best thing for her and Hope . . . and for their grandmother."

"If only you could have brought them here, then maybe she'd forgive me, but you sent her to Roseland. I bet there isn't one rose there or anything nice." I was so upset that I let Raven go and rolled over on my stomach. Burying my face in my pillow, I sobbed while Mom rubbed my back and tried to comfort me.

When I could talk calmly, I asked, "Do you really think they'll be all right at Roseland?"

"I'm sure they will be. Please try not to worry about them, honey. You'll just make yourself feel worse."

"Where is Roseland?"

"Up in the mountains. Somewhere west of Hagerstown, I think."

"Is that far?"

"About fifty or sixty miles, I guess." Mom stroked my forehead. "When you feel better, do you want to go and see them?"

I nodded. "If Daphne wants me to."

Mom shifted her weight, as if she were about to get up. "Don't go." I grabbed her hand. "Stay a while, just till I fall asleep."

She smiled. "Is there anything I can get you?"

"No, just you. You're all I want," I mumbled.

For three days I felt too sick to think about anything, even Daphne. My body felt as if someone had beaten it all over with a baseball bat, and my throat was so sore I could hardly talk. All I did was sleep, drink orange juice, and take aspirin. On Sunday I felt well enough to sit up and watch television, and on Monday I ate dinner downstairs with everyone. Mom decided that I would probably be able to go back to school by Thursday.

"Maybe you should call Tracy and see what's going on in your classes. She could tell you what you've missed and help you get caught up," Mom suggested.

Reluctantly I dialed Tracy's number. I hadn't heard from her since she'd walked home with me from the village center. I was afraid that Michelle and Sherry might have convinced her that I was as strange as Daphne.

The phone rang once, twice, but just as I was about to hang up, Tracy's little sister said, "Hello?"

"Hi, Kelly, is Tracy there?"

"Just a minute." With an ear-splitting clank, she dropped the phone. "Tracy!" Kelly bellowed. "It's for you!"

"Who is it?" I heard Tracy yell.

"I don't know, some girl. Not Michelle."

"Tell her I'll be there in a minute."

"She's in the bathroom," Kelly yelled into the phone, then dropped it again, almost deafening me for life.

After a while, Tracy said, "Hello?"

"Hi, it's me."

"Jess, how are you? When are you coming back to school?"

"Thursday, I think. Have I missed much?"

"Just the same old boring stuff." While Tracy filled me in on the details of book reports, math tests, and history projects, I tried to analyze her tone of voice. She didn't sound bored or angry or disgusted, so I hoped that things were still all right between us.

"You won't have any trouble catching up, Jess. You're such a brain and all." Tracy popped her gum and added, "Did you know Daphne is in Roseland?"

"How did you find out?"

"Mr. O'Brien told us. He thought some of us might want to write to her or something."

"Do you think anybody will?"

"No. I'd kind of like to, but I don't know what to say. I was thinking maybe I'd send her a funny card or something."

"She'd like that."

"I guess you've written to her."

Embarrassed, I doodled little spirals on the pad by the phone. "I haven't yet. I guess I felt too bad." I hesitated, then asked, "Are Michelle and Sherry mad at me?"

"No, I don't think so. In fact, Michelle said to tell you she was sorry she upset you. She didn't mean to make you cry." Tracy popped her gum again and added, "Don't let her bother you, Jess. Michelle doesn't mean half the dumb stuff she says."

"I'll try to remember that." I grabbed a Kleenex and blew my nose. "Well, thanks for telling me what's going on at school, Tracy. I think I'm going back to bed. I still feel kind of crummy."

"I'll see you Thursday, okay?"

"Okay." After I hung up, I felt a little better about everything. At least Tracy was still friendly, and, if she were telling the truth, Michelle and Sherry weren't going to say or do anything too horrible to me.

Rescuing Raven from the corner Snuff had backed him into, I carried him up to my room and crawled into bed. I turned out the light and lay in the dark listening to Raven's wonderful rumbling purr. In the corner of my room, the moonlight dimly illuminated my dollhouse. I thought of Princess Heatherfern standing at her window and Cragstar poring over his books in the tower. They were still waiting for Sir Benjamin to come home, but I

163

knew he wasn't going to return. Like Daphne's father, he was gone for good.

"You might as well be brave and face the truth," I whispered to the mice. "Daphne was right about happy endings. They just don't happen in real life."

Sixteen

When i went back to school, nobody said anything about Daphne except Mr. O'Brien. He caught me in the hall after school and started asking me questions.

"I'm so worried about Daphne," he began. "Have you talked to her since she went to Roseland?"

Avoiding his eyes, I shook my head. "It's a long-distance call." Even to me that sounded like a feeble excuse.

He frowned. "I didn't think of that. Well, have you written to her?"

Again I shook my head. "I've been really sick," I mumbled.

He sighed. "I'm sure she'd enjoy hearing from you, Jessica. You were the only real friend Daphne had here." He sounded puzzled.

"It's all my fault she's in Roseland, don't you know that?" Angrily I felt tears fill my eyes. I didn't want to cry in front of Mr. O'Brien, especially not here in the hall where anyone might walk by and see me. "Daphne doesn't want to hear from me. She hates me for telling my mother, I know she does!"

Mr. O'Brien shook his head. "I don't think Daphne could possibly hate you. Please write to her, let her know she has a friend."

After promising Mr. O'Brien that I would write to her, I edged away from him toward my locker. All the way home I composed letters in my head, but when I sat down at my desk, a blank sheet of stationery in front of me, all I could write was "Dear Daphne." Nothing more.

Days went by. Every night I promised myself I'd write the letter in the morning, but I never did. The more I delayed, the guiltier I felt. To make myself feel better, I told myself that Daphne despised me, that I was the last person she wanted to hear from, that she would probably tear a letter from me to pieces without even reading it.

Then, about three weeks later, Mr. O'Brien told our English class that he had an announcement to make.

"I'm proud to tell you that Daphne's and Jessica's book won first prize in the county Write-a-Book contest."

Everybody clapped and smiled at me. When the room was quiet, Mr. O'Brien added that "The Mysterious Disappearance of Sir Benjamin Mouse" was now on display in the exhibit hall at the Board of Education building.

"In June, the winners are invited to attend a special awards banquet. I'll have more information on that later, Jessica."

After class, Mr. O'Brien stopped me. "Would it be

possible for your mother to drive you out to Roseland so you could give Daphne the good news in person?"

"I guess so," I said.

He tipped my chin up, forcing me to look at him. "I'm sure she doesn't hate you, Jessica."

"But I let her down. I broke my promise."

"Go see her, take her the good news about the book." He smiled. "I'd go myself, but I'm sure she'd rather see you."

That Sunday Mom drove me out to Roseland. It was a long ride through the rolling farmland of western Maryland. Mom had no problem as long as we stayed on Interstate 70, but as soon as she found herself trying to navigate the winding country roads that led to Roseland, she got lost. We had to stop at three gas stations and a funny little store to ask directions.

Finally we drove over the crest of a hill and saw an official-looking green sign pointing the way to Roseland. Following the arrow, Mom turned into a narrow driveway, winding uphill through trees tipped now with green.

"What happens if someone comes in the other direction?" I looked ahead at the narrow road. It wasn't wide enough for two cars, and I couldn't see a shoulder, just trees crowding right up to the rutted asphalt.

Mom grinned. "Just hope no one leaves before we get there."

At last we left the woods behind. Ahead of us, at the end of a circular drive, was Roseland. It was a huge stone house sitting on the top of a hill. Behind it the mountains loomed, almost as blue as the sky.

"What a beautiful place," Mom sighed. "It must have been someone's home once a long time ago."

I stared at the building, but all I saw was its grimness. Bristling with fire escapes, it looked like a prison to me. I was sure Hope and Daphne didn't think it was beautiful.

"Do you want me to come in with you?" Mom nosed the car smoothly into a parking place marked VISITORS ONLY.

I shook my head. "I think I'd rather see her alone, if you don't mind."

Mom smiled. "I'll just walk around the grounds, then. It's a beautiful day, and I brought a book." She waved a copy of *Your Second Marriage: Make It Work* at me.

"Okay. I'll see you later, then." As I started to open the car door, Mom leaned toward me and gave me a kiss. "Do you think Daphne'll still be mad?" I asked her.

"I'm sure she'll be happy to see you, Jessica. She knows you wanted to help her."

I nodded, but I wasn't absolutely positive that Mom was right. Waving to her, I walked slowly across the parking lot and followed a sidewalk to the front door. Big beds of daffodils and tulips did their best to brighten the approach to the house, but even their cheerful colors couldn't mask its institutional appearance.

Nervously I stopped in front of the closed door. Was I supposed to ring a bell or knock or just walk in?

While I hesitated, the door opened and a woman carrying a briefcase stepped out. She noticed me and smiled. "Can I help you?"

"I came to visit a friend of mine," I whispered.

168

Stepping aside, she held the door open. "Just cross the lobby and tell the woman at the desk whom you want to see."

"Thank you." I crossed the threshold, the door thunked shut behind me, and I found myself in Roseland.

The lobby was large and high-ceilinged. I suppose it had once been a lovely room, but now its walls were painted an ugly shade of pale green and the floors were covered with scuffed, dingy linoleum. A Coca-Cola vending machine stood against one wall, and an exit sign glowed dimly in a dark hallway.

Sprawled in one corner was a group of kids watching television. They glanced at me and then turned back to the cartoon. Other kids, in groups and alone, lounged on ugly green couches and chairs. Some were talking, a few were reading, but most of them were just sitting there, looking bored and unhappy. I didn't see Daphne or Hope.

Self-consciously, I crossed the room and stopped in front of the desk. The woman sitting there was reading a magazine, and I had to clear my throat twice to get her attention.

"Yes?" She looked annoyed at being interrupted.

"I'm here to see somebody, a friend of mine." I tried to keep my voice from shaking. I don't know what scared me most—talking to this frowning woman or the prospect of seeing Daphne.

"Name?"

"Mine or hers?" My voice defeated me and quavered like a child's.

"Hers, of course." The woman looked at me as if

she were dealing with a new low in human intelligence.

"Daphne Woodleigh," I whispered, and then I had to repeat it twice and spell it before she understood whom I wanted to see.

With a sigh heavy enough to steam my glasses, she flipped through a file. "Room 205-A. Shall I buzz her?"

I stared at her. "I guess so."

The woman buzzed twice, but nobody answered. "Well, she's not there." She looked at me, waiting for me to tell her what I wanted to do next.

"Do you know where she is?"

She shrugged, causing her large bosom to ripple under her blouse. "Sunday's a free day. She could be anywhere. You want me to page her?"

Embarrassed at all the trouble I was obviously causing this person, I nodded. "If you don't mind."

The woman sighed again, indicating she minded very much, and picked up the phone. "Daphne Woodleigh," she said, her voice seeming to come from the ceiling, "please come to the lobby. Daphne Woodleigh."

I glanced down the hall, but there was no sign of Daphne.

"If she doesn't answer, she's outside somewhere," the woman said. Then she picked up her magazine and bent her head over the article she was reading.

I waited for what seemed like a very long time, shifting my weight from one foot to the other, conscious of the woman's annoyance. I was sure she wanted me to thank her and leave, but I stood by the desk, thinking that Daphne would appear at any moment.

Finally I heard a familiar voice piping shrilly over the din of the television set. "Jessica, Jessica!" A skinny little body barreled into me and two small arms circled my waist.

"Hope, how are you?" I hugged her as tightly as I could. She felt tiny and fragile, like a baby bird. "What's the matter?"

Her small body shook with sobs. She was crying too hard to talk, so I led her over to one of the couches and sat down. Climbing onto my lap, she buried her face in my shoulder and continued to weep.

"What's wrong, Hope?" I whispered. "Is it awful here?"

"I miss my grandmother, I want to go home," Hope sobbed. "And Daphne won't talk to me, she won't talk to anybody."

I held her tighter and let her cry herself out. When she finally calmed down, I stroked her hair and gave her a Kleenex. "There. Do you feel better now?"

She looked up at me and tried to smile, but her chin was still wobbly from crying and her lips quivered. "I'm glad you came. I missed you."

"I should have come sooner." I felt very remorseful.

"If you'd waited till next week, we wouldn't be here any more."

"Where are you going?"

"To Maine. They found some of Mommy's relatives, and they came to see us last week. They went back to get things ready for Daphne and me, but they're coming again next Friday."

"Are they nice? Do you like them?"

Hope nodded and gave me a better smile. "Alice is pretty, and Dave has a big beard that tickles me and he's funny. He makes me laugh."

171

"You'll be happier when you go to Maine, won't you?"

Hope nodded. "But I'll still miss Grandmother. And you, Jessica."

I hugged her. "I'll miss you too, Hope." Gently I slid her off my lap and got up. "Do you know where Daphne is?"

"She has a secret place she goes to. She won't let me come with her, but I followed her once, so I know where it is."

"Do you think she'd talk to me?"

"I don't know."

"Is she mad at me? Does she hate me for telling my mother?"

"I don't know." Hope reached into her pocket and pulled something out. It was Baby Mouse, looking a little shabby. Hope walked him up and down my arm and said, "Squeak, squeak."

"Has Daphne said anything about me at all?"

Hope shook her head. "She never talks, Jessica. Not to anybody. Not even to Alice and Dave."

"She must hate me." Sadly I watched Hope playing with Baby Mouse. I wondered if I should go find Mom and leave without even trying to find Daphne. But instead I asked Hope if she would show me Daphne's secret place. If she wouldn't talk to me, I'd talk to her. Maybe she would at least listen.

Seventeen

HOPE LED ME outside, past the daffodils and tulips, to a nicely mulched path that wound off into the trees. Away from the big stone house, it was very quiet. The new leaves made lacy shadows on the ground, and the sunlight gleamed on Hope's hair. The air had a fresh, damp smell, filled with the odors of leaf mold and earth and growing things.

Being in the woods reminded me of the times that Daphne and I had climbed the trail leading to our rocks above the Patapsco River Valley, and I found myself walking quietly, hoping the three deer would slip out from among the silent trees.

"How is Raven?" Hope asked, pulling me back from my daydream about the deer.

"Oh, he's fine, he really is." I smiled at Hope. "He's the best kitten in the whole world. You should see him. He's getting so big, and he sleeps on my bed every night and purrs whenever I pick him up. I'm so glad you remembered to give him to Mom."

Hope looked pleased. "I knew he'd be a good cat. Does Snuff like him?"

I shook my head. "But she ignores him. She isn't mean to him unless he bothers her. Like when he jumps on her tail or tries to eat her food." I laughed. "But he has enough sense to run when she starts hissing."

"Alice and Dave have two cats and a dog," Hope said. "They're very nice, but I'll still miss Grandmother's cats. They took them all to the pound, did you know that?" Hope's eyes filled with tears and her chin wobbled. "They're probably all dead now."

I gave her a hug. "Maybe not. They could have been adopted or they could have run away. Try not to think about it, Hope."

We walked on silently. Birds sang all around us, and not too far from the path, a creek ran noisily over stones. Finally Hope stopped and pointed ahead. In a clearing was a bench, placed to overlook a view of rolling hills and mountains. Sitting on the bench was Daphne, her back to us.

"You go tell her I'm here," I whispered to Hope.

She nodded and ran toward her sister. At the sound of her footsteps, Daphne looked up, then turned and stared at me.

Before I could say a word Daphne jumped up and ran away from me, leaving Hope calling after her, "Wait, Daphne, wait!"

Dodging around Hope, I followed Daphne. Instead of staying on the path, she dashed into the woods, taking a zigzag course downhill through the trees.

Wordlessly I pursued her, tripping, stumbling, but keeping her in sight. Each breath I took stabbed my

chest with pain, but I didn't stop to rest. I was determined to catch her.

Finally I saw her leap a creek, catch her foot on
something, and sprawl face down in the dead leaves
carpeting the ground. Expending the last of my energy,
I jumped the creek and tumbled to the ground beside
her.

We were both too out-of-breath to speak, but she
glared fiercely at me, as a fox run to ground must glower
at the hounds surrounding it. My sides heaving, I returned her stare. Now that I had caught her, I didn't
know what to say.

"What are you doing here?" she gasped at last.

"I wanted to see you, I wanted to talk to you," I
whispered.

She started to stand up, but I grabbed her arm and
pulled her back down. We crouched in the dead leaves,
staring at each other. Suddenly Daphne collapsed. Face
down on the damp ground, she began to sob.

Cautiously, I reached out and touched her shoulder.
When she didn't pull away from me, I patted her gently,
but I didn't say anything. I let her cry, just as Hope had
cried.

Finally she grew quiet, but she didn't look at me.
Or speak.

"Daphne," I said softly. "I know you must hate me.
I'm sorry about what happened in the store. I know I
should have helped you, but I couldn't. I didn't know
what to do."

When she didn't respond, I went on. "I had to tell
my mother, I had to. I was scared that something awful
was going to happen."

She still didn't say anything. She just lay there, her head cradled in her arms.

Then I thought about what I'd said. "Something awful happened anyway, didn't it?" I sighed. "I'm sorry, Daphne, I'm really sorry. Please don't hate me."

My words hung between us like balloons over the heads of comic strip characters. Somewhere in the trees a bird sang. All around us green shoots thrust up through the dead leaves. Looking closely at one, I realized that it was a baby fern curled into a tight spiral, waiting for a little more warmth before it dared to open itself to the world around it.

"Hope says you're going to Maine to live with some of your relatives," I said softly.

Still no response. Gently I lifted the hair hiding her face. "I've missed you a whole lot, Daphne," I whispered.

Daphne sat up then, but she turned her face away, and her hair tumbled down between us once more.

I stared at her silently. The bird sang again, but this time another bird answered. They called back and forth, their voices as clear and beautiful as drops of water falling into a still pool.

"Do you want me to go away?" I asked.

With one hand, she cleared some leaves from a baby fern and poked gently at its coiled stalk.

"I'll leave if you want me to." I stood up slowly, hoping she'd ask me to stay.

Daphne looked up at me then, her face paler and thinner than it had been before. Her eyes were bright with tears. "Did Hope tell you that Grandmother died?"

176

Shocked, I shook my head. "No. She just said she missed her."

Returning her attention to the fern, Daphne said in a low, expressionless voice, "She died a couple of weeks ago. They'd put her in a hospital. She had pneumonia, but she got worse because she hated it there. She wouldn't eat anything and she wouldn't cooperate with the doctors or nurses."

Daphne glanced at me, then looked back down at the ground. "They let me go see her," she went on, "but most of the time she didn't even know who I was. The day she died, though, she looked me straight in the eye and said that everything was my fault. She said that if Hope and I hadn't come to live with her, she'd still be at the farm and Daddy would be there with her. She said I'd kept him away."

Daphne bent her head and began to cry. Kneeling beside her, I patted her back again. "She didn't mean that, Daphne. She was old and sick. She wasn't in her right mind. You did everything you could."

Daphne shook her head. "No, she was right. I'm a horrible person." She stretched the fern out and watched it roll back up, as tightly curled as ever. "You'd hate me if you knew what I was really like."

"No, I wouldn't, Daphne." I pushed my glasses up onto the bridge of my nose and waited for her to go on.

When she continued to sit there silently, coiling and uncoiling the fern, I added, "You're one of the nicest people I know. Do you think most sisters would take care of Hope the way you did? Josh would have run

177

away and left me if we'd had to live with somebody like your grandmother."

"Sometimes I did want to run away." Daphne looked at me, her eyes full of worry. "But it's not Hope I feel bad about. It's Grandmother. Sometimes I hated her, Jessica. Sometimes I used to lie awake in that cold house and wish she were dead. I'd listen to her breathing in the dark and I'd wish she'd stop!"

Her eyes dared me to tell her how nice she was now that I knew the truth about her. "What kind of person has thoughts like that, Jessica?" Her voice was shrill, her face fearful.

"Maybe everybody," I whispered.

Shuddering, I remembered something I'd done when I was seven, something I was ashamed of still. "When my father told me he was getting a divorce, I told him I hated him and wished he was dead. I screamed it at him, Daphne, and then I ran upstairs and locked myself in the bathroom. I wouldn't come out till he was gone."

I pulled my jacket closer about me. "After he went to California, I used to tell people he was dead. I thought that sounded better than admitting he had left my mother and gone all the way across the country. And I used to wish it were true, Daphne."

"But he didn't die," Daphne said, "and Grandmother did, that's the difference. When they told me she was dead, I was glad, Jessica! I knew I'd never have to see her again, I'd never have to go back to that house, I'd never have to hear her talk about Daddy like he was still alive."

She clenched her fists. "Then, while they were standing there, waiting to see what I was going to do, I started to cry. And I cried and cried and cried. I cried harder than I did when Mommy died, but it wasn't because I was sad. It was because I felt so guilty and bad and horrible."

"Oh, Daphne, you're not horrible, you're not."

"But to hate my own grandmother, to be glad she's dead! She couldn't help being the way she was, Jessica. She didn't mean to scare us." Daphne stared at me. "Only an awful person would feel like that."

I shook my head. "Please don't talk that way, Daphne. You did your best to take care of Hope and your grandmother. And she was scary, I was terrified of her. Anybody would feel the way you did."

"Do you really think so?" Daphne gazed at me thoughtfully, her brow wrinkled.

I nodded.

"And you still like me? Even now that you know what I'm really like?"

"You're the best friend I've ever had."

Daphne smiled then, just slightly and not for very long. "I'm glad you came, Jessica."

"Me, too." We stood up and brushed the dirt and leaves off our jeans.

"Where did Hope go?" Daphne looked around.

About twenty feet away, we saw Hope sitting on top of a boulder, peering at us like a little wood elf.

"Come on." Daphne jumped the creek and ran up the sloping ground toward Hope. "Hey, you, come down from there!" Laughing, she grabbed Hope's foot and gave it a gentle tug.

"Help, help, it's the giant troll girl!" Hope squealed and pulled away.

Daphne growled menacingly, and I tackled her from the rear, "I'll save you, elf girl! Run, run for your life!" I shouted to Hope.

While Daphne and I wrestled, Hope ran off through the trees. Laughing hysterically, Daphne and I jumped up and ran after her, growling and roaring like wild things.

We chased each other through the woods, changing identities and sides, until we were exhausted. Finally we collapsed on a moss-covered rock, gasping for breath. As our breathing returned to normal, the three of us gazed quietly into the delicate green woods, each thinking our private thoughts. It was as if we were lying again on our rocks above the Patapsco.

"Oh, Daphne," I said, breaking the silence, "I almost forgot to tell you! Our book won first prize." I handed her the note Mr. O'Brien had given me for her.

Smoothing the paper, Daphne read it. "That's wonderful!" She smiled, and her mouth, her eyes, her whole face looked happy. "But how can I go to the banquet? I'll be in Maine then."

"Maybe your relatives would drive you down here and you could all stay at our house for a few days. Wouldn't that be great?"

"Me, too?" Hope asked.

"Of course you, too!" I grinned at Hope. "We couldn't leave you and Baby Mouse out, could we?"

"That's a wonderful idea, Jessica." Daphne smiled again. "I hope Alice and Dave will bring us."

"They have to," I said. "The book would never have won if you hadn't drawn the pictures."

"But I couldn't have drawn the pictures if you hadn't written the story," Daphne said.

I shook my head. "You thought of a lot of the ideas. Even the ending. It's your book, Daphne. I couldn't have written it without you."

Daphne looked pleased. "I still think it's equal, half yours and half mine."

Hope snuggled up against Daphne and smiled. "It's part mine, too. Baby Mouse wouldn't have been in it if I hadn't been there."

Daphne and I laughed. Then from somewhere behind us we heard a bell ring.

Hope jumped up, looking close to tears. "Oh no," she wailed, and threw her arms around me.

"What's the matter? What does that bell mean?" I asked.

Daphne slid off the rock. "Come on, Hope." Turning to me, she said, "It means free time is over and the visitors have to leave. We'd better go back."

As we walked silently down the path, Daphne and I looked at each other. I knew that my face was just as sad as hers.

"You will come in June, won't you?" I asked her as we neared the end of the woods.

She nodded. "If Dave and Alice will bring me."

"They must!"

"There's your mother," Hope said.

Mom waved to us. "Hi, girls." Smiling, she greeted Hope with open arms. "You've grown, haven't you?"

Hope laughed. "I've gained three pounds. They have good food here."

Mom turned to Daphne and gave her a hug. "You look fine, too."

Daphne drew back, embarrassed, I guess, by Mom's hug. But she smiled.

"We're going to Maine next week with Alice and Dave," Hope said. "They have a big house near the ocean and a dog and two cats."

"That's wonderful, Hope." Mom looked at Daphne, her eyes full of questions.

"Alice is my mother's second cousin," Daphne said. "The social worker found her."

"They came to see us, and they want us to live with them. They have one little baby, but they want some big girls like Daphne and me, too." Hope clung to Mom's hand and danced about, laughing. "They're fixing up our bedrooms and everything. We'll be able to see the ocean from our windows."

"I'm so happy." Mom scooped Hope up and gave her a kiss.

Slowly we walked across the parking lot toward Roseland. A tiny sliver of moon and a single star hung in the pale sky just above the treetops, and the windows of the house glowed with lamplight. All around us, people were calling good-bye. Headlights swept across our faces as cars left the lot.

"There's the second bell," Hope said sadly.

Daphne and I looked at each other. "I wrote my address at the bottom of Mr. O'Brien's note," I said. "Will you write to me?"

"Of course." Daphne smiled at me.

"Do you promise?"

She nodded solemnly. "May the sky fall on me, may

the earth swallow me up, may the waters of the sea sweep over me, if I don't write to you, Jessica," she said gravely in her best Cragstar voice. "That's a special threefold oath. It's very sacred."

"May the same three things happen to me if I don't write to you." I grabbed her hand and shook it hard. "I'll see you in June."

"In June," Daphne promised. She pumped my hand vigorously as Hope threw herself at me, pulling my face down for a big, wet kiss.

"Good-bye, Jessica." Daphne released my hand and turned toward Roseland. "Did you really mean what you said?" she asked suddenly, her face swinging toward me in the dusk.

I nodded, knowing immediately what she meant. "Yes, you're the best friend I've ever had."

"You, too," she said. Then she was gone, running toward the glowing windows of Roseland with Hope behind her, looking back and waving.

About the Author

MARY DOWNING HAHN was born in Washington, D.C., and now lives in Columbia, Maryland, with her husband and two daughters. She works as a children's librarian in Prince George's County, and previously taught art in a junior high school and English at the University of Maryland. She has written *The Sara Summer* and *The Time of the Witch*, and is currently at work on a fourth novel.